THE DEVIL

Cards of Love

ASHLEY JADE

First published in USA, November 2018

The Devil

Cover Design: Lori Jackson at Lori Jackson Design

Editor: Ellie McLove

The Devil

"Hell is empty and all the devils are here."
—William Shakespeare, The Tempest

Please pay attention to the Card description.
As it will be your only warning.

The Devil Card

The Devil (XV) is the fifteenth trump or Major Arcana card in traditional Tarot decks.

Meaning:
The Devil is the card of humanly desires. It represents being seduced by the material world and physical pleasures. Also living in fear, domination, and being caged by an overabundance of luxury. Discretion should be used in personal and business matters.

The Devil in Love:
The Devil also indicates sexual interests such as bondage, bisexuality, and fetishes. In its darkest form, the Devil can represent sexual slavery and obsession.
They must have you at all costs.

Depiction:

The Devil card depicts the devil as the ancient goat-god Dionysius, shown sitting on his throne while watching over a male and female captive chained naked to the podium on which the Devil sits. The lovers are slaves to their desire, urges, and raw passions. Each has small horns on their head, similar to the devil—a sign that they are becoming more and more like the devil the longer they stay. Both have tails—a further symbol of their animalistic tendencies and raw instincts.

They appear to be held against their will, but upon closer inspection, you'll notice the chains around their necks are loose.

They are free to go whenever they like.

Please Note:

This book is a *prelude*

And it's best you go in blind.

Warning:

There are no heroes in this story.
Only devils

Prologue

Obsession is a peculiar thing. Unlike other emotions, it doesn't happen instantaneously. Instead, it grows slowly—like a fungus invading the dark corners of your mind, contaminating your every thought.

Until suddenly—you're sick. Infected with an incurable disease.

The object of your neurosis is all you can focus on.

You spend every waking moment fixated on them. Questioning what they're doing. Who they might be thinking about.

Your evenings are spent conjuring images of them with their current lover. And your nights are spent dreaming about what it would be like to see them again.

Touch them. Taste them. Have them at your mercy…fulfilling every single desire and urge pumping through you.

Until finally…you can't take it anymore. The lines between fantasy and reality become blurred and you start meticulously plotting strategic steps to enact your encounter.

Looking back, that's the point my obsession spun out of control.

I should have maintained my distance. But I couldn't.

Eleven years spent away didn't dilute my craving—it only made it fester. My sickness was far too advanced and was only getting worse. My need for him was far too strong to be ignored or contained.

So, I continued planning. Seeking the perfect crack in his life to slip through undetected. Once I had it…the only thing left to do was wait for the perfect moment to strike.

But the thing about plans is…
They never work out like you expect them to.
Sometimes life throws you an innocent, young, blonde…curveball.

Chapter 1
EDEN

"Are you excited for the annual Black Hallows Masquerade Ball this Saturday?" the reporter, interviewer, *royal pain in my ass* asks.

It's all I can do not to roll my eyes. This chick has officially earned her spot on my shit-list for not only sticking me in the same vapid box as every other eighteen-year-old girl but failing to do her research.

I plaster a fake smile on my face. "Super pumped."

Negatory. The only thing I'm excited for is watching Netflix and munching on the raw cookie dough I have a date with.

Not looking at all put off by my snark, she continues, thrusting her iPhone at me to record my response. "Is there a special boy in the picture?"

It's too late to diffuse the question. There's already a brutal flush creeping from my toes all the way up to my hairline.

Reporter bitch looks like the cat who ate the canary. "I knew it. Pretty girls like you never go unnoticed, do they?"

There's an unmistakable hint of pettiness in her statement, and I know without a doubt this interview is about to go downhill fast.

Something I probably should have realized sooner given she has yet to ask me a single question about Cain's campaign for mayor. In other words, the reason we're having this interview in the first place.

I look around, but her next question forces my attention back to her. "Just between us girls, is it weird having a father who's only a few years older than you?" She fans herself with the paper in her hand. "Lord knows I couldn't live under the same roof with Black Hallows' most eligible bachelor. Not without sleeping in his bed every night." Her gaze turns calculating. "Then again, rumor has it, affairs with older men aren't exactly out of the question for you."

The implication makes me fidget. A rookie mistake.

"He's my stepfather." Squaring my shoulders, I find my resolve. "And he's only Black Hallows' most eligible bachelor because my mother is dead, you heartless bitch."

She starts to speak, but I stand up. "This interview is over."

"What's going on in here?" a deep voice that sounds like melted chocolate over gravel barks from the other room.

I meet his dark eyes when he enters, refusing to look anywhere else for fear my legs will turn to jelly and the reporter will have a field day. Too late…my control is waning. Today Cain's wearing his green tie that brings out the subtle flecks of gold in his orbs. Sweet baby Jesus in a manger. I'm so screwed.

Tossing my long blonde hair over my shoulder, I shrug and head for the exit. "Nothing."

A touch to my elbow halts me and just like that—I'm spilling my guts.

"This asshole from the Independent Chronicle came here to remind me that my mother croaking made you Black Hallows' most eligible bachelor…and because the town still hasn't found a new whore to point fingers at, I must be spreading my legs for you."

Like a good politician about to face a scandal, Cain releases me and turns his attention to the reporter, looking outraged. "That's absurd. She's my deceased wife's daughter."

My heart, the bruised and battered thing twists in my chest and I look at the reporter. "You can go fuck yourself." My stare snags him again. "You too."

A faint shiver of delight zips through me when I see his annoyance simmering beneath the surface. *Good.*

Maybe now he'll understand how I've been feeling ever since the *incident.*

The one that ended with him discarding me like I was nothing more than a dirty rag, then come right back around and use me whenever it's convenient for him.

Just like everyone else in my life.

His jaw tics. "Where's David? I thought we all agreed he'd supervise you during these?"

"That's funny." I gesture between us. "We didn't agree to anything. You told me some reporters wanted to interview me this week and said not to speak to anyone without him present."

"Eden," he grinds out, and I curse myself for wondering if that's how he'd grunt my name if we finished what we started that night. "Where is he?"

I give him a big smile. "I told him to grab some lunch." My smile falls. "You know, since I'm not a fucking child who needs a babysitter."

With that, I march upstairs to my bedroom.

"What newspaper did you say you were from? Because you'll be cleaning out your desk by the end of the day," Cain booms from the living room. His voice lights every nerve ending of mine on fire, even from so far away. Until I hear the next words out of his mouth. "For fuck's sake, my wife's body isn't even cold yet. What kind of person comes into someone's home and says that shit to a kid who's still mourning her mother."

Locking the door behind me, I fight the urge to laugh. My mother's been dead for over a year now, and Lord knows I haven't spent more than a second grieving the woman who treated me like her life's greatest mistake instead of her daughter.

Neither has Cain.

Despite him ripping the reporter a new one, anyone with a pulse knows their marriage was one hot steaming pile of bullshit.

He was twenty-five and she was thirty-nine when they got

hitched—which made me—who was only fourteen at the time—closer to his age than my mother.

But given her own campaign focused on family values when she ran for District Attorney four years ago—and she had no family—other than the daughter who caused a huge scandal that year—she needed to find someone to fill the gaping hole my sperm donor left in our family portrait.

Enter Cain Carter—not one to pass up a good opportunity, even in the face of gossip and outrage—he married her. Most likely because— scandal or not—she knew all the right people. People who ironically enough, got him to where he is now.

Running for mayor and presumed to win. Which will officially make him the youngest mayor Black Hallows has ever had.

Well, as long as there aren't any scandals in the next eleven days.

I know he's wanted this for a while now, but to be honest; I have mixed feelings. Half my heart wants him to win because I know it's a stepping stone to his real dream—becoming president one day. But the other half wants him to lose so it gets rid of at least one obstacle between us.

Then again, if he loses, who knows what will happen to me. As of tomorrow, I'm a legal adult, which means he's no longer under any legal obligation to take care of me.

Shortly after my mother died in a car accident, Cain disclosed his plans to run for mayor and gave me two choices. Either I could end up a homeless teenager on the street, because my cunt of a mother didn't leave me a dime. Or I could stay with him and he would take care of me, provided I did everything he said, played the part of the good little stepdaughter, and didn't cause any waves during his campaign.

It was an easy choice. I've been in love with Cain since the moment I laid eyes on him…despite meeting him while I was at my lowest.

Unfortunately for me, he's as straight-laced as they come,

appears to give a shit about my well-being most days, and would never cross that line.

Except for that one night.

Chapter 2

EDEN

Three Weeks Ago

"Didn't know you were in here."

I startle at the sound of his voice even though I heard the front door open followed by his footsteps.

Fumbling for the remote, I put the show I was barely paying attention to on pause and look at him.

The light from the television illuminates his tall and toned form as he rests against the entryway and I fight back a shiver.

If he didn't enjoy politics so much, I'm positive he could have had a successful career as a model. He's an intriguing combination of rugged and boyish good looks. Light brown hair cropped close in a style that's suitable for business. Big brown eyes that are full of determination—like he's always working toward the next big goal. And his chin, which is clenched in irritation more often than not, has the sexiest dimple smack dab in the center of it.

However, my absolute favorite feature of Cain's are his lips. The man has the kind of lips women from all over the world go under the knife for. They're full and sensuous, turning up at the corners ever so slightly to give him a perpetual smirk—like he knows how bad I want to kiss them.

"It's Saturday night, shouldn't you be hanging out with your friends?"

I inwardly flinch, not because of his cool tone or the slight slur coming from the booze he must have consumed tonight, but the fact that he knows damn well I don't have many friends. Make that *any*.

I'm pretty much the town's pariah, thanks to an incident that occurred when I was fourteen that led to my mother pulling me out of regular school and me continuing my studies at home.

Even now, the sting of embarrassment is so sharp my breath catches. I never meant for anyone to get ahold of the letters I wrote my seventh-grade teacher, Mr. Delany.

Ever since I was little, I've related to adults more than people my own age—something Mr. Delany seemed to understand—and we formed a friendship.

However, my private thoughts about him were never supposed to see the light of day. Those letters were for my eyes only.

Unfortunately, once Tricia Rosenberg found them…they were for everyone else's eyes too. Given my expressive language and graphic details of everything I wanted him to do to me…half the people in town thought he was some kind of child molester.

The other half thought I was a teenage Lolita…trying to ruin a good man with a good family because I came from a broken home and had daddy issues.

Needless to say, my life quickly became a living hell. I was bullied by my peers and verbally abused by the adults who were supposed to protect me.

My mother—already a prominent lawyer, played the offensive at first, claiming her young daughter was taken advantage of—no matter how many times I tried to tell her nothing ever happened between us and they were just stupid fantasies of mine.

However, things only got worse when I made the mistake of meeting Mr. Delany in the middle of the night to apologize for all the trouble I caused him. His wife showed up shortly after we did, and to say the shit hit the fan would be putting it mildly.

My life was one giant cluster fuck after that, but throughout it all, I maintained both mine and Mr. Delany's innocence. In the end, I shouldn't have gone through the trouble because Mr. Delany—just like every other man in my life—turned his back on me. He ended up telling everyone who would listen that I was a mentally ill stalker who was obsessed and blackmailing him because I was angry he turned down my advances.

Since there really was no disputing my fascination with him thanks to the letters, the town had a field day playing judge, jury, and executioner. Especially after it came out that Mr. Delany had ties to some important politician people admired.

My mother had no choice but to save face and her career by claiming her teenage daughter had severe psychological issues, and she decided to do the right thing and send me away so I could receive the proper treatment.

I've been stuck inside this house ever since. A prisoner of rumors, poor choices, a selfish mother, and the inner workings of my own peculiar mind.

It's only recently that I've started to interact with people outside my home again—thanks in part to Cain and my therapist's, David, help.

I'm still not able to venture outside most days—not even to the mailbox—because my anxiety and fear forbid me. But at least I'm finally able to hold conversations with those who come here.

The irony. Most girls my age can't wait for the freedom to explore the universe on their own terms. Yet I want nothing more than to stay trapped inside these four walls forever...because I know first-hand what a cruel place the outside world can be.

"Oh, that's right," Cain muses, bringing me out of my thoughts. "You're not really much of a people person. Are you, princess?"

"Rough night?" I throw back at him because I hate when he intentionally provokes me. I'm pretty sure he's not too fond of it either.

Yet, we've done this little song and dance so many times I'm starting to lose count. Maybe we secretly resent one another because deep down we both want what we can never have. Maybe these taunts and underhanded digs we hurl at each other are our sick way of keeping our real feelings at bay since we know we can never act on them.

Or maybe…I'm just wishful thinking and fantasizing like I did with Mr. Delany all those years ago and Cain can't wait for my next birthday so he can get rid of me for good.

God knows his attitude lately makes it seem that way. Which means I need to be on my best behavior because I'm certain I'll die if he kicks me out. Not only because I'll be broken-hearted, but I don't have what it takes to make it on my own. I can barely make it down the driveway without breaking out in a sweat and having a panic attack.

Slipping his tie off his neck, he releases a long sigh. "You might say that."

I sit up straight as he walks toward the couch, watching his every move. "Want to talk about it?"

He makes a dark mocking sound. "I'm good."

Tucking a strand of hair behind my ear, I look around, unsure of what to do or say.

"Am I making you anxious?" The mocking tone in his voice is replaced by genuine concern. "Want me to leave?"

"Yes—no."

He raises an eyebrow, amusement lighting his face. "That really clears things up."

I laugh, my body relaxing a little with the action. "Yes, you're making me anxious." When he turns to leave, I quickly add, "But I don't want you to go." I point to the contents on the coffee table. "The popcorn's burnt and the soda's warm, but it's still edible."

He gives me a boyish grin as he takes a seat on the ottoman where I'm resting my feet. It's strange he would pick the seat closest to me when he usually does the opposite. Another inch or so and we'd actually make contact.

I feel stupid when he sticks his hand in the popcorn bowl and I realize he took the seat closest to the refreshments…not me.

He makes a face. "This is awful."

I shrug. "Hey, I warned you."

Pushing the bowl away, he reaches for a can of soda and takes a large swig. "Fair enough. But why would you eat burnt popcorn in the first place? Why not throw it out and make yourself a new bowl?"

I pick at a loose string on my t-shirt. "Well, if I threw it out and started over, all my time and effort would have been for nothing. And if I made a new bowl of popcorn, I'd have to go through the whole monotonous process of waiting and listening for the kernels to pop at just the right time…something I already screwed up once tonight." I chew on my thumbnail. "Two things I hate are wasting my time and having to do something over again because I didn't do it right to begin with."

He runs his hand over his chin, looking bemused but not saying a word.

"What?" I prompt after another moment passes.

"Nothing." When I give him a look, he says, "We're a lot alike is all." Another long sigh. "I don't like the thought of wasting my time or starting over again, either."

"I guess that's why you've been so on edge about the election." I clamp a hand over my mouth when I realize I said that aloud. "Sorry."

"Don't be." His hand accidentally grazes my foot when he rests it on his knee and my breath steals. "One of my favorite qualities about you is how blunt and honest you are."

My lips twitch. "Wow, would you look at that—a politician who admires honesty."

The rumble in his chest makes my heart take flight only to dive right into the pit of my stomach a second later when he grabs my foot playfully and gives it a squeeze. "Smart ass."

I swallow the ball of nerves lodged in my throat when he places my foot in his lap and looks at me. "David says you're making progress."

I nod. I hate when he brings up my therapy. It only reminds me how messed up I am and how there's virtually no chance of us ever being together.

It also reminds me that our time is coming to an end. I'm not an idiot. I know Cain only insisted I start intensive therapy to deal with my agoraphobia and other issues after my mother's death because he wants me out of his life when I turn eighteen.

Can't say I blame him. Who in their right mind would want to keep taking care of a headache they didn't create? Cain's already done more for me than my biological mother ever did.

And while I don't think I'll ever be able to go outside without feeling anxious about people gossiping and saying horrible things behind my back…I finally have hope that one day I'll be normal.

Still doesn't change the fact that I'm absolutely petrified Cain is going to set me loose soon. No matter how much he deserves to live his own life.

"What's wrong?"

"Nothing." He gives me the same look I gave him earlier and I cave. "I'll be eighteen in three weeks."

I watch his Adam's apple bob. "I know." His pinched expression tells me he's been thinking about it as much as I have.

My stomach knots. I can practically hear the clock ticking. "I think I'm gonna be sick."

I go to get up, but he places my other foot on his lap and rests his forearm on top of my ankles, locking me in place. "What's going on with you?" I open my mouth, but he growls, "Don't tell me *nothing*."

Tears prickle my eyes. I have no idea how to say this without sounding like a desperate nutcase, but I'm so scared I'll take the risk.

"I'm not ready to leave yet. I need more time." I meet his eyes. "I know it's a lot to ask. I know it's not fair to you. I know I'm leftovers—"

"Leftovers?" He looks at me like I've sprouted another head. "Eden, what the hell are you talking about?"

"Aren't you kicking me out when I turn eighteen?"

"No."

I look at him skeptically. "You sure?"

He chuckles. "I'm pretty damn positive."

I fold my arms across my chest. "Oh." Half of me feels like a fool…and the other half is grateful nothing's changing. "Thanks."

"Not exactly sure why you're thanking me, but you're welcome." He gives his head a shake. "I should probably let you get back to whatever it was you were doing."

He starts to get up, but a red mark on his collar catches my eye and my stomach rolls with a violent lurch. "Where were you tonight?"

I'm not stupid, I know Cain's had sex with other women after my mom died. Heck, I'm almost positive he was having sex with other women *before* she died given the two had absolutely zero chemistry.

I've just never been confronted with the evidence like this before.

"I don't think that's any of your business."

He's right, it isn't…but my heart didn't get the memo. It was bad enough I had to witness him with my mother—I don't think I can handle the thought of him being involved with someone else.

If I had it my way, I'd be the dirty little secret he takes to his bed every night instead of his doting little stepdaughter.

If I had it my way, I'd be the one fulfilling every single want and need of his so he'd never have to look elsewhere.

If I had it my way, Cain would feel for me a fraction of what I feel for him.

But Cain's never seen me that way and I don't think he ever will.

His morals and ethics won't let him.

Not unless I do something to shake them up a little.

Leaning back against the pillow, I dangle my feet on his lap again, intentionally stretching out my slim, t-shirt clad frame. "Come on, Cain. I thought we were friends."

If he notices the provocative tone my voice has taken, he doesn't comment on it.

As usual, he remains silent. Jaw clenched. Eyes hard.

But he's not leaving…which means there must be a small part of him that likes being around me.

"Have you been seeing her long?"

He glares at me. "I'm not talking about this with you."

"Why not?" I ask coyly. "I mean, I'm pretty much legal now. Surely we can have an adult conversation…right?"

His eyes follow the fingernail I'm sliding up my torso. "I'm not talking about my sex life with my daughter."

"We both know I'm not your daughter, Cain."

My nipples pebble when his gaze locks on my bare legs. "No, you're not." Torment etches his features. "Still doesn't make it right."

My heart is practically beating out of my chest. This is the first time he's ever looked at me this way, but if I play my cards right…it won't be the last time.

Slowly, I slink my foot up his thigh. "Doesn't make what right? We're friends. Friends talk about sex."

He snorts. "I'm not talking about sex with someone who hasn't even had her first kiss yet."

I don't know whether to be flattered he thinks I'm so virtuous or offended. "I've been kissed before."

"When?" His eyes narrow. "You told me nothing happened with that pervert—"

"Not him."

"Then who?"

The whisper of jealousy in his tone makes my insides swoop.

I bite my lip and wiggle my toes a little, making sure they brush a certain appendage that's growing thicker by the second. "I'll tell you mine if you tell me yours."

"No." The pad of his thumb traces the arch of my foot and I shiver. "You go first."

"Fine. My first kiss was with a girl I used to hang out with."

He eyes me skeptically. "What was her name?"

"Viola Cesario." I fold one arm under my head—an intentional move that causes my t-shirt to rise, exposing my white cotton panties. "I used to go to her house after school, and one day while we were doing our math homework—she asked if she could kiss me to see what it was like." I draw in a leisurely breath and his eyes drop to my breasts. "I was a little nervous, but she was so gentle with me." I lick my lower lip. "To this day, I still remember how her mouth tasted like bubble gum." I give him a wry smile. "We kissed for so long I thought our lips would fall off. If it wasn't for her older brother walking in on us, they might have."

His throat bobs on a swallow. "What did he say when he caught you?"

My smile grows. "He asked us to do it again." This time, I'm not subtle when I brush his now bulging erection with my foot. "But he had one special request."

Cain makes a low noise in his throat. "What was that?"

I walk my fingers down the length of my body, stopping when I reach the band of my underwear. "He asked her to kiss me here."

His cock pulses beneath me. "What did you say?"

I make a lazy circle over the fabric, inching closer to my clit. "What do you think?"

He zeroes in on the damp spot forming beneath my fingers. "I think you're a girl who's easily corrupted by all the bad things in life."

I slip two digits inside my panties, catching the wetness on them. "It's kind of sweet you think I'm so innocent."

His expression turns pained with lust and I know I've got him right where I want him. "That's because you are."

Removing my hand, I hold up my glistening fingers. "Well, if I'm an angel, what would that make you?"

"Right now?" He leans in, his mouth a mere centimeter from

the fluid I'm teasing him with. "The Devil." He sucks my fingers into his mouth and groans. "Because one taste of you won't be enough."

Butterflies fill my belly, but a vicious wave of arousal chases them all away when he starts stroking me through my underwear. "Tell me what happened next."

I have to pinch myself to make sure this is actually happening and it's not another fantasy of mine. "She said she didn't know what to do...so her brother...he..."

"He what?"

His knuckle grazes my clit and I suck in a breath. "He offered to show her."

"Fuck." He squeezes his erection through his pants. "Did they taste your pretty pussy at the same time?"

"Yes." I'm so turned on I can barely breathe. "It felt so good."

"I bet it did." A shiver runs through me when he moves my panties to the side and slides his finger past my swollen lips, easing his way in. "God, you're so tight." A wet sound fills the room as he drives through my slickness and I buck against his hand. "So fucking tight."

With a grunt, he drops to his knees. "Spread your legs."

The moment I do, he buries his face between my thighs and starts lapping at me like an addict who's consuming his next hit.

"Did they kiss you like this?" he grunts between long licks that have my legs shaking.

I start to speak, but the sound of his zipper cuts me off. Heat rises to my cheeks when I look down at his cock. It's thick and veiny, the shiny pink head teasing his navel. It's crazy finally seeing what I've been fantasizing about for years.

Another finger enters me, stretching me so much it almost hurts. "You didn't answer the question."

"Yes," I moan, and he kisses a languid path up my slit, rewarding me. My nails dig into his shoulders when his kisses turn frantic, his tongue hitting all the right spots. "Please don't stop."

He sucks my clit into his mouth and I rock against his jaw, seeking more.

"That's it," he rasps as he begins fucking me with his fingers. "Be a good girl and come on my face."

His lips fasten onto my clit and the pressure between my legs detonates, sending me off. "Oh, God."

Cain holds my gaze as I whimper and writhe, moaning his name like it's the last word I'll ever say as he consumes my orgasm.

I lay there breathless, so far gone I'm not sure I'll ever come back. I knew it would be good with Cain, but the real thing far exceeded my expectations.

With a smirk, he removes his fingers from my pussy, smears my cum on his dick, and pumps it nice and slow.

Then he stands, positioning his hard-on directly in front of me, giving me a privileged front-row seat to the show. I'm so transfixed all I can do is stare, watching in fascination as a pearly drop forms on his tip.

Curious, my tongue comes out for a quick taste and he groans, working his hand up and down his shaft rapidly. "Open."

When I do, he winds my hair in his fist and thrusts, shoving his dick so far down my throat I gag. "Swallow."

That's the only warning I get before his body tenses and his release fills my mouth. There's so much it starts dripping down my chin, but I do my best to get down every drop.

I'm so focused on the task I don't catch the shift in Cain's demeanor.

Not until he pushes me off him, looking about as guilty as a priest who committed murder. "Fuck."

"What—"

A string of curses leaves him as he tucks his dick inside his pants. "This was a mistake."

Wiping my mouth, I push to my feet. "What's wrong?"

He gestures between us. "This can't happen again."

"Why—"

"You know why, Eden."

I cross my arms over my chest, feeling so vulnerable I could cry. "I'm—"

"Don't be sorry." His jaw bunches and he backs away. "And don't be a fucking liar."

I shake my head. "I don't—"

"*Viola Cesario*," he spits.

Shame barrels into me so rapidly my knees buckle. I should have known Cain was a Shakespeare fan, considering I know almost everything else about him.

He runs a hand down his face. "I'm a good guy, Eden." His expression turns stern, like a parent explaining something to a small child. "But I'm still a guy. Don't tempt me like that again, because I'll only end up breaking your heart, and you need someone to make sure you're…" His voice trails off and he shrugs helplessly. "Don't hurt the only person who ever gave a fuck about you, okay?"

"I'm not trying to hurt you. I would never. I love—"

"No, you don't." His eyes flicker with rage and he points a finger at my face. "Stop telling yourself shit like that before you fuck up both our lives." He kicks the coffee table, sending the popcorn and soda flying across the room. "I'm so close to winning this election and one step closer to where I want to be." He punches the wall with his fist, looking so out of sorts tears prickle my eyes. "I'm so fucking close to getting everything I ever wanted…and I won't let you or anyone else ruin it."

With that, he stalks off…leaving me there with a broken heart and the lingering taste of him in my mouth.

I was so close to getting everything I ever wanted too.

Chapter 3

EDEN

I'm watching reporter bitch drive off when my phone pings.

My heart flutters and I click the *Temptation* app so quick I'm surprised my fingers don't go up in smoke.

I never in a million years thought I'd join a site that's primarily used for hookups and cheaters, but curiosity got the best of me when I received an e-mail two weeks ago telling me my membership was now activated and they were charging me two hundred bucks.

Normally I would have discarded it, but two things stopped me. One—it was addressed to Cain. And two—the PayPal email they were withdrawing the funds from was *mine*.

Needless to say, I was livid. I hit reply and told them the person they were looking for was my stepfather—not me. I figured I'd never hear back from them and I'd have to tell Cain to take care of it, but to my surprise, the app developer wrote back almost immediately, apologized for the mix-up, and then offered me a free yearly membership for all the trouble.

When I explained that—according to their terms and conditions—I wasn't even old enough to use the app since I wasn't eighteen yet, he said he wouldn't tell anyone if I wouldn't.

Then he sent me the private link to download the app.

As far as dating sites go, it's pretty basic with a straightforward layout. There are a few chatrooms for people to connect and socialize and a private messaging option.

And other than the age requirement, there are only two rules. One—you can't have a profile picture. And two—you can't use your real name.

You can only disclose those things in a private message at your own discretion.

I didn't have any interest in using it, but approximately two hours after joining *Temptation*—I received a message from some guy who lived in Black Hallows, was twenty-nine, involved in a career he wasn't comfortable revealing…and knew tons of things about me.

According to his profile, he first joined the site a few hours before I did.

In other words—it's obviously Cain. Although he still won't admit it outright. Probably because the things we talk about on here aren't always *politically correct* and he's nervous about me or the app developers outing him.

It's like a whole other life between us inside these chats. A glimpse of how it could be.

But I'm still angry at him for dissing me before.

Devil: How's my girl?
AngelBaby123: Shouldn't you be working? Or you know, busy grieving your deceased wife?
Devil: Can't. I'm too busy thinking about a gorgeous blonde. A gorgeous blonde who's legal in two more hours. :-P

I can't help but laugh as I type my response.

AngelBaby123: Thinking of all the ways you're going to corrupt and defile me, are you?
Devil: Always.

Devil: But enough about my devious intentions. How does my girl want to celebrate the best day in the world?

I get comfortable on the bed.

AngelBaby123: Movies with my lover. Double chocolate chip cookie dough.
Devil: I thought you were turning eighteen. Not eighty.
AngelBaby123: That's hilarious coming from you, Grandpa.
Devil: More like Daddy. ;)

I bite my lip.

AngelBaby123: So are you finally admitting it's you?
Devil: I admit nothing. But if I was going to reveal my identity, I wouldn't do it in a message.
AngelBaby123: Hmm. Then would it involve finishing what we started three weeks ago?
Devil: Maybe. Why don't you send me a little something to jog my memory?
AngelBaby123: Like you don't already have enough nudes of me.
Devil: What can I say? I'm a greedy bastard who can never get enough of you or your fantastic tits.
Devil: Why don't you be a good girl and venture farther south for me this time.

My cheeks heat. I've sent him topless pictures—minus my face—because I'm not dumb enough to put that into cyberspace, but I haven't gone further than that.

Devil: You don't have to.
AngelBaby123: How about this…I'd rather show you in person.

I chew my thumbnail, a nervous habit of mine, and wait for him to respond.

Cain's weird when it comes to our little chats. He won't discuss them in person and the one and only time I made the mistake of alluding to talking to him late at night, he looked at me like I sprouted another head.

I've concluded that him not talking about us outside the chat, or admitting it's him inside the chat is his way of making sure he can trust me. I think he wants to ensure I can keep a secret before we take it any further. I'm guessing it's why he concocted this whole plan in the first place, even though he won't admit it.

AngelBaby123: You there?

When he doesn't answer after five minutes, I send him another message.

AngelBaby123: Is everything okay?

Devil: Sorry, baby. Had to take care of something. Where were we?

AngelBaby123: It's cool. I was about to take care of some things myself. Catch you later.
Devil: You're upset.

A little.

AngelBaby123: No.
Devil: I forgot how sensitive you are and how much you hate being ignored.

Cain's perceptive as it is, but it's downright eerie how much better he can read me through a phone screen.

AngelBaby123: I'm fine.
Devil: Okay, tough girl. But just so you know, I'm the same way.

AngelBaby123: I hate how you do that.
Devil: Do what?
AngelBaby123: Know me better than I know myself.
Devil: Why do you hate it?
AngelBaby123: Because it makes me feel weak. Like you have the upper hand and we're on an uneven playing field.
Devil: I wasn't aware we were playing a game.
AngelBaby123: We're not. I just hate feeling like you know more about me than I know about you.
Devil: What do you want to know about me?

I type and delete my response over five times before I have the courage to send it. I know almost everything there is to know about Cain…except for one thing that's been bugging me ever since I heard about it.

AngelBaby123: Where were you the night the fire happened that killed your family?
AngelBaby123: Are you there?
AngelBaby123: Hello?

His username turns gray…informing me he signed out of the app.

Chapter 4
CAIN

The last thing I need right now is a scandal.

Correction—the last thing I need is to go up to her bedroom.

Yet, here I am…walking up the stairs. Heading straight for the Devil's playground.

One mistake three weeks ago turned Eden from my sick little fantasy …to my greatest liability.

It was hard enough not to think about her before that night… but it's been impossible not to think about her since.

I'm so fucked.

She's lying on her bed when I walk in—phone in hand, a cute little pout on her pretty face; like she's waiting for someone to respond.

She's been preoccupied with her phone a lot over the last two weeks, which wouldn't be weird for any other girl her age, but Eden has never been what you would call *normal.* She has a lot of issues that prevent her from making and keeping friends.

She has a lot of issues that make people take advantage of her.

Which is why crossing the line was wrong on all accounts. She might be eighteen in a few hours, but I'm supposed to be the adult in this situation.

Then again, Eden's more mature than most adults in this town. Unlike them, she's not the type to spread false stories or go out of her way to hurt anyone.

Which is probably why her mother resented her so much. Karen was incredibly smart, sure; but she wasn't a lot of other things. Things like kind, loyal, and charismatic. Things that make a person likable.

In other words, all the things Eden is.

I clear my throat to get her attention, fighting a bout of annoyance because I'm used to having it the moment I walk into a room.

She narrows her eyes. "Did you need something?"

Eden is sweeter than sugar when she wants to be, but she's also sassy as hell when she's upset. It's all I can do not to laugh because Eden being mad is the equivalent of a baby cub roaring.

She's all bark and no bite.

"I got rid of the reporter." I stick my hands in my pockets so I'm not tempted to touch her. "I also made a few phone calls. Let's just say she won't be conducting any more interviews."

Thanks in part to my family and my deceased wife's contacts, I have a few connections. Although few is putting it mildly. I know enough of the right people I'm able to run for mayor before I turn thirty…despite all the rumors and black marks of my past.

Which is why I relate to Eden so much. I know first-hand how poisonous Black Hallows can be. I know how it feels to have an entire town talk about you and your family behind your back but never to your face.

But unlike Eden, who hasn't built an outer shell because her mother kept her hidden away to protect her own precious reputation—I was able to rise above it and come out on top.

However, we'll both fall down if anyone ever finds out what transpired between us.

It's bad enough everyone in Black Hallows already speculates about our relationship, given how close in age we are—and Eden's past, thanks to that inappropriate teacher of hers.

It's a shame he wasn't put behind bars, because it was obvious to anyone with a pulse he was grooming her and only a matter of time before he did something heinous.

It really goes to show it's not what you know in this town, it's *who* you know. That pervert happened to be the nephew of a powerful judge, which had my wife—the DA who only earned her position because of her own manipulative ways—backing down and turning on her own kid.

The day Karen died, I promised myself two things. One—when I became mayor, I'd piss on her grave for being such a cunt to Eden. And two—I'd help Eden overcome her demons any way I could.

But it's hard to do that when everyone around you thinks you must be sticking your dick in your stepdaughter.

It's even harder when they're not exactly wrong...because you've had the urge to make those rumors a reality for the last year.

With a sigh, I walk around her bedroom. Being so close to her when she's lying on a bed isn't good for my self-control. "I shouldn't have pushed you to do those interviews. I'm sorry."

Given people in town haven't seen Eden in years because her disorders prevent her from stepping outside, I thought arranging a few interviews with the local media here at the house would be a good thing.

For her…and me.

But it backfired once they started publishing pictures of her.

Younger Eden was already a Lolita in their minds. But older Eden is everything wives' nightmares and men's wet dreams are made of.

Like temptation and sin wrapped up in a beautiful bow.

Long blonde hair, big blue eyes, pouty lips, curvy ass, legs for days, and a rack that makes a man curse and thank God every Sunday at his local church.

And don't get me started on the tight holy grail between her creamy thighs.

Fuck.

Blowing out a breath, I force myself to stop thinking with the wrong head. Screwing my stepdaughter is out of the question. No matter how much I want to.

And after this weekend, hopefully the gossip—and my hunger—regarding me and Eden will clear up for good.

Eden doesn't know yet, because I haven't the heart nor the want to break it to her—but I have an arrangement with Margaret Bexley. Or rather, her governor father, who happened to be an old friend of my father's.

Milton Bexley's not only filtering a shit-ton of money into my campaign on the low, he's not so secretly hoping I'll take his place one day since he doesn't have any sons, and his only daughter Margaret is more interested in being a Stepford wife to a politician than she is in actual politics.

On paper, the situation is perfect. Eons better than the arrangement I had with Karen—the one I stupidly accepted due to being young and impulsive.

I just have to tread carefully because perception is everything in this town. If I jump into a relationship with the governor's daughter too quickly, people will think I'm only doing it for political gain.

But if I continue living as a widow with my gorgeous stepdaughter who's locked up like a princess in a tower…it will only perpetuate gossip and make them uneasy.

And if they have any room for doubt about my character when it's time to vote, I won't have theirs.

I've worked my ass off for this for a long time now, waiting for the perfect moment to toss my hat into the ring. I couldn't run while still married to Karen, due to more than half the people in town hating her. Unfortunately, divorcing her before running would have been career suicide since Karen wasn't the type who would take me leaving her lying down. She'd already threatened me with one hell of a smear campaign revolving around Eden if I ever ended things and ran for mayor. She wasn't keen on her show dog husband having more power than she did.

The fact that she was willing to drag her own mentally fragile daughter into the spotlight after the same town already chewed her up and spit her out just to ruin *me* speaks volumes.

Then again, Karen was ruthless.

Almost as ruthless as…

The hairs on the back of my neck stand on end and I grit my teeth.

Not a day goes by that I'm not reminded of Damien King, given his obsession with me ruined my life twelve years ago.

Last I heard, he was a successful hedge fund investor with more money than God and was living halfway around the world on some exotic island…which suits me perfectly fine.

Because if I ever see him again…I can't guarantee I won't kill him.

There's a reason people in this town refer to him as the Devil.

The man is pure evil. A psychopath if there ever was one.

"Cain? Are you okay?"

Eden's voice brings me out of my thoughts and I look down at my hands which are clenched so tight they're white. "Fine."

I turn to leave, but her next sentence halts me. "Is this how it's going to be between us now?"

I can't have this conversation with her. "I don't know what—"

"Yes, you do." She sits up in bed. "You've barely spoken to me in person since that night, and when you do you talk right through me like I'm another item on your business agenda you need to cross off."

"I—" I'm at a loss for words. There are so many things I want to tell her, but she won't understand or accept any of them.

She won't understand how I'm trying to save us both by not throwing any more logs into the fire between us.

She won't understand that if we get involved and we're found out…I'll resent her for ruining my second chance and she won't have anyone else to take care of her.

She doesn't know I've already made the mistake of getting involved with someone I shouldn't have and paid the ultimate price for it…and I won't let history repeat itself.

"Why do you keep messing with my head?" Her voice wobbles. "I'm not something you can use."

"Eden." I wait for her to look at me because I need her to get this through her head for once and all. "I'm sorry I hurt you, but that night was a mistake. Please try and understand."

She draws her knees up to her chest. "Was it a mistake because you're scared of people finding out…or because you don't want me?"

There's no easy way to navigate her question. If I tell her the former, she'll think there's hope when there's not. But if I tell her the latter, I'll hurt her.

Cupping her cheek, I tell her the only thing I can. "The reason doesn't matter. The result is still the same."

"No, it's not. What if we didn't live in Black Hallows anymore? What if we left and—"

"No," I growl because she's not comprehending what I'm saying and it's starting to remind me of someone I'd rather forget. "No matter where we go, people will know who I am because that's what my job calls for. And sooner or later they'll figure out who you are too."

"I guess that leaves secret option three." She closes her eyes and sighs. "I'm not important enough to give up politics for."

She's not wrong. Politics have been in my blood since the moment I took my first breath…literally. My father was a senator and my older brother had just been accepted to Harvard and was on the same political track I was when they died. Even my mother—who I don't remember much of because she passed away when I was three—was a successful campaign manager for government officials.

While all the other boys I grew up with were interested in sports and parties, I was interested in student council and the debate team, trying to make a difference and put my mark on the world.

My father, who ruled with an iron fist, both figuratively and physically; had my future political career mapped out since I was a child. It was the only thing we ever agreed on.

"I don't think a relationship works well when one has to sacrifice an integral part of who they are to make the other happy." I cradle both her cheeks. "Besides, do you really want to be kept hidden away for the rest of your life? That's no way to live, Eden."

"What if that's exactly what I want?"

"You only want it because it's all you've ever known." I run my thumb over her cheekbone. "There's a whole big world out there for you to discover. So many experiences waiting for you."

"I don't want the world," she whispers and the muscles in my chest draw tight. "I only want you. All I've ever wanted was you."

Christ, this girl. She has a way of looking at me like I'm personally responsible for making the sun rise and set every day.

She has a way of making me feel like I'm her God. And fuck if there's not a small part of me that doesn't revel in it.

"You never wished me happy birthday."

The change of subject throws me and I check my watch. "Technically your birthday isn't for another ten minutes." I wink. "I'm not that old. I still have a few more years before senility sets in."

She starts to laugh, but a scowl twists her features. "Too bad the stupid masquerade ball is tomorrow night."

"I know."

It's always the Saturday before Halloween. Normally I'd skip it because balls aren't really my thing, but it's eleven days before the election. Which means I have no choice but to show up. The two weeks before an election is the most crucial and it's just one of the many appearances I have lined up.

Eden tilts her head to the side, studying me intently. I should probably tell her about Margaret since we're on the subject…but I don't have the heart to break hers when her birthday is mere minutes away and she's already so upset.

"I don't suppose there's any chance of you skipping it?" She looks so hopeful it kills me. "We could watch movies, or—"

"I can't." When her face falls, I add, "But you could go."

I know it's a long shot given all her struggles, but I'm hoping she'll give it some real thought before turning me down.

Besides, there's no reason Eden shouldn't go if she wants to. It's not like I'm planning on screwing Margaret in public tomorrow night.

And even if that were the case, it wouldn't matter. The second Eden walks through those doors, she'll be surrounded by guys. Guys her own age who would undoubtedly do anything for her attention.

Jealousy hits me like a fist to the gut, but I shake it off with a roll of my shoulders. I have no right to be jealous. *She's my forbidden fruit.*

Therefore, she deserves to find someone who can give her all the things I can't.

Pride fills me when I peer down at her. The adorable look of concentration on her face tells me she's actually considering it. This is a huge step in the right direction.

"I don't have a dress."

"Use my credit card and buy one."

She chews her bottom lip, contemplating. "It's too late to order express shipping online."

"You can go shopping for a dress in the morning." When she winces, I say, "Or I can send Claudia to the store to pick one out for you."

Claudia is my campaign manager and personal assistant.

"Claudia's seventy-three," Eden grumbles. "She'll end up picking out some psychedelic flower-child frock that will make people talk about me even more."

Eden has a point. Claudia is great at what she does—but she's also a self-proclaimed hippie with very questionable fashion choices.

"Write down what you want. Color, size…girl shit."

The corners of her lips turn up. "Girl shit?"

I shrug helplessly because I'm clearly out of my element and she giggles. "Okay, fine. I'll write down my girl shit."

For a second I think I misheard her, but sure enough; she's picking up a pen and pad off her nightstand.

Only to place them back down a moment later. "I don't think I can do this. I'm so sorry."

Her shaking hands and tear-stained cheeks chip away at the

barrier I put up between us.

Crossing a boundary I know I shouldn't, I pull her into my arms. "Don't be sorry. They have one every year." I tip her chin. "You'll go to one when you're ready."

She sniffs. "What if I can't?"

"You will."

"How can you be so sure?"

"Because there are two types of people in this world. Those who are capable of greatness, but don't bother trying. And those who still try even though they're not capable of greatness."

Her face screws up. "I do—"

"You're neither." I wipe her tears away with my thumbs. "You're the type of girl who can do anything she sets her mind to and succeed."

She leans her forehead on my chest. "You really think so?"

"I know so. You don't even have to try. Everything you want in this world is already yours." She trembles and I run my knuckles down the nape of her neck, watching goose bumps erupt over her delicate flesh. "All you have to do is reach out and take it."

She looks up, her blue orbs darkening with lust. "What if everything I want is standing right in front of me?"

My dick twitches and I mutter a curse. I'm not sure I have enough willpower to keep turning her down. Not when she's pressing her hot little body against me like she is now.

But I have to. The lines between us are becoming blurred again. "Eden—"

She places her finger over my lips while her other hand falls to my zipper. "I know." Slipping her hand through the opening of my pants, she runs a finger over my thickening erection. "But according to the clock on the wall, it's officially my birthday." I grunt when she wraps her hand around me and squeezes. "And I really want a birthday kiss." She smiles coyly and drops to her knees. "Or should I say—to blow out my candles."

I'm a sick man because those innocent words dripping with dirty intentions have my resolve diminishing and my dick rock hard.

I'm pretty sure this is what standing outside the gates of hell must feel like.

"Eden," her name comes out in a low groan as she takes me into her mouth.

This is wrong. So wrong.

Wrong. Wrong. Wrong.

"Suck it faster."

I'm so fucking sick.

Sick. Sick. Sick.

"Good girl." I wind her hair around my fist as bolts of pleasure caused by her hot little tongue punch through my body. "Suck me just like that."

Gagging sounds fill the room as she goes to town on my dick, taking me in swift long strides.

Bracing an arm on a nearby chair, I watch as she pleasures me, somehow looking even better than all the fantasies I've had starring her over the last year.

Pink full lips stretched around my shaft. Cheeks hollow from sucking. Blue eyes glassy from my cock constantly hitting the back of her throat.

In other words—utter perfection.

And God help me because it makes me want to find out what she'd look like if I was balls deep inside her.

She picks up her pace and I rock into her mouth. "Fuck."

I should end this, but the devil on my shoulder whispers that since I'm already going to hell, I might as well enjoy it and take everything she's offering.

And despite being a grown man who knows better, I listen.

Yanking her upright, I shove her on the bed.

Her eyes widen in surprise. She looks so innocent it sends another pang of want straight to my dick.

I hover over her slim frame. "You drive me fucking crazy." Running my nose along her temple, I inhale her flowery scent. "What am I gonna do with you?"

Her chest heaves, drawing my attention to her perfect tits. "Anything you want."

"That so?" With a grin, I shove my hand underneath her shirt and cup her tit in my hand. They're every bit as firm and ample as I thought they'd be. "Take this off and let me see them."

She makes quick work of removing her top and I make my way down her torso, pausing to lick and suck every inch of her toned abdomen.

Circling her belly piercing with my tongue, I look up at her. I feel like a goddamn teenager again because all I can do is stare at her full breasts and peach colored nipples.

Her cheeks turn pink and she starts to cover herself, but I shake my head. "Don't you dare." With a grin, I push her jeans down a little, revealing those razor-sharp hipbones. "We're not done."

My cock throbs when I see her smooth, bare pussy peeking out. "Not even close." I pop open the button on her jeans and graze the length of her slit. "So wet." Stretching my fingers, I open her. "So pretty."

I plant a kiss on her sensitive clit and she utters a throaty moan that goes straight to my balls. "Do you have any idea how bad I want this?" I circle the sensitive bud with my tongue. "How much I want to make you come all over my dick."

"Do it," she rasps, goading me. "I told you, I'm all yours."

With a groan, I tear her jeans off and position myself between her thighs. I'm about to thrust, but I feel her body tense underneath me.

"You okay?"

"Yeah." The pink of her cheeks deepens, and she draws in a shaky breath. "I just haven't…I've never done this before so I'm a little anxious."

I freeze, the awareness of what we're about to do hitting me like a steel bat to the prick. I suspected she was a virgin, but hearing her confirm it seconds before I'm inside her, makes this whole thing feel even more…wrong.

I look down at my cock nudging her entrance, wondering how the hell I let myself get so far down the rabbit hole.

I care about Eden. Really fucking care about her. In two very different, very *conflicting* ways.

But one side is winning out right now.

"I'm on the pill." She smiles nervously. "You don't have to worry."

I stand up and tuck myself back into my pants. "I'm not taking your virginity."

"What?" She sits up. "Why? Everything was perfect."

"No, everything was not perfect." I pick her clothes up off the floor and hand them to her. "You deserve more than this."

"But I love you, Cain." The space between us tightens as we lock gazes. "I love everything about you." Her lower lip trembles. "Even when you hurt me, I *still* love you."

There's a part of me that knows I'll regret what I'm about to say the moment the words are out of my mouth, but it's the only way. This can't keep happening. We're spiraling out of control and if I don't stop it...lives will be ruined.

Just like last time.

"No, you don't. You only think you do because you never leave the house and you don't know any better. You're a sweet, beautiful girl. But this thing…this *sick* shit brewing between us is over for good."

Hot tears fall down her face. "But you love me too." The tears fall faster, and I honestly hate myself for making her hurt like this. "I *know* you love me."

"I do love you, Eden." Then before hope can rear its ugly head, I add, "But not in that way. I love you like a f—"

"Don't," she chokes out, shooting me a look that would turn a weaker man to stone. "Just get out."

"Eden—"

She grabs a vase off her nightstand and I watch as it shatters against the wall. "Get the fuck out, Cain."

I walk to the door, my heart in my throat. "I'm sorry."

"No, you're not." She buries her face in her hands. "You never are."

Chapter 5
EDEN

I clutch my chest as pain slashes through me. It's so severe I lose my breath. So brutalizing…I swear I can actually feel my heart breaking into a million tiny pieces.

Like I'm dying slowly with every beat of the shattered organ.

And yet, if God were to offer me one final wish before my soul departs the earth—I know exactly what I'd wish for.

The same thing I've wished for every night for the past four years.

I'd wish for Cain Carter to love me the way I love him.

But I know now that will never happen…and it's not because he doesn't love me. It's because he doesn't love me in that way.

He doesn't *want* to love me the way I love him.

Because he equates loving me with something sick and wrong.

An evil sin.

And deep down I know I should let him go and try to find a way to move on, but I can't.

Because the fucked-up thing about love is—just because the person you love doesn't love you back…it doesn't stop you from loving them.

It only makes you love them even more, makes you hold on a

little tighter…because your love is the only thing that still tethers you to him.

And if the thread were to snap. If the foundation you built were to ever crumble. You're left with nothing.

Sometimes the only difference between love and obsession is a broken heart.

Chapter 6

DAMIEN

Flecks of gold, blue, green, and white dash back and forth in front of my eyes. There's little more tranquil in this world than sitting in the dark watching fish swim under neon lights.

It's a pity the click-clack of heels across the marble floor of my office disrupts my meditation.

"Good thing I don't care about my job as a reporter, because the interview went exactly like you said it would." The young woman—Jodie—huffs out a breath from behind me. "I was halfway here when I got the phone call I was fired."

My lips twitch. I knew Cain had a soft spot for his stepdaughter. Can't say I blame him. She is…special.

"You'll be well compensated for your trouble." Standing, I sprinkle some food in the tank. They haven't been fed in two days, so they'll be pleased.

"Find out anything interesting about Eden?"

"You mean other than her being a typical high society bitch whose shoes cost more than my rent?"

"Jealousy is such an unattractive trait."

"So is ignoring someone you want information from. Are you

going to turn around and look at me at some point, or are you planning on giving me my money telepathically?"

"That depends."

"On?"

"If looking at you is a better view than the one I have now."

I glance down at the small security screen displaying our exchange.

It's not.

The girl's mouth drops open. "Wait, are you…was that? I mean, I'm totally down to fuck. You're Damien freaking King. I saw your picture on your website and nearly pissed myself." She puts her hands on her hips. "But I'm no prostitute."

"Here's a tip. Don't walk into my office late at night expecting to be paid for a job you haven't completed. My time is valuable—so you can either use that mouth of yours to tell me about the interview and leave with a check in your hand…or use it to suck my cock and leave with nothing but my cum on your face. The choice is yours."

"Geez." She shuffles her feet nervously. "Sorry."

I pinch the bridge of my nose when she fetches a stick of gum from her purse.

The girl is testing my patience, and if she's not careful I'm going to strip her and fuck her little asshole…right before I drown her in my tank. "Jodie."

I don't have to look at the security screen to know she jumps. "Sorry, I have to chew gum when I'm nervous. Anyway, I didn't talk to her for long. And to tell you the truth, she's kind of a brat."

Exhaling, I sit down in my seat. "How so?"

"Well, when I asked her if she was excited about the party tomorrow night—you know, before I brought up her being a whore—she gave me an attitude."

Probably because she doesn't venture outside, you idiot.

"Oh, crap. Hold that thought. I can't believe I almost forgot." She claps her hands like she's about to share the latest news with some girlfriends. Which is exactly why I hired her in the first place. Young women leave out nothing when disclosing gossip.

"You were right. He's totally screwing her."

"What makes you so sure?"

I know Cain wants to, but I wasn't aware they crossed that line…yet.

"You mean besides the fact that he ran into the room like a white knight when I made her upset?"

"I'm sure he was just concerned about his daughter."

Or scared Eden slipped up about their inappropriate relationship.

I lean back in my chair and smirk. *If she'll disclose it to a stranger on the internet, what's to stop her from telling anyone else?*

She laughs. "Yeah, concerned about his image. He touched her when he walked in the room—nothing sexual. However, the second she told him I insinuated they were hooking up, he jumped back like she was made of lava." She snorts. "Then he started acting all holier than thou. Like the thought of fucking his centerfold stepdaughter was something that never crossed his mind before."

"Interesting. How did Eden respond?"

"Oh, homegirl was pissed." She snaps her gum. "Although I don't know why. If I was doing him—and I totally would because he's hot as fuck—I'd be more than happy getting dicked down by him every night and spoiled rotten during the day." She rolls her eyes. "I know she's a blonde, but she can't seriously be dumb enough to think it will ever be more than sex between them. I mean, *hello*—not only is he about to be mayor, but everyone knows he married and fucked her mom."

She chews vigorously. "But yeah, that was basically it." She drums her fingernails on my desk. "So, now that you have all this info, what are you planning on doing with it? Obviously, there was a reason you wanted me to ruffle her feathers and spy on them."

Tuning her out, I draw my attention to the fish again.

They look so innocent swimming around in captivity. So content now that I've fed and taken care of them.

So pretty. *Just like Eden.*

She taps her foot. "Are you going to stare at those fish the whole time I'm here?"

"No."

Pressing a button on my chair, I release the divider between the main tank and another one that's hidden out of view. The one containing a very angry, very *hungry* red-bellied piranha.

In less than a minute…all my pretty fish are dead.

They never saw it coming.

I spin around in my chair. "Take off your clothes."

Chapter 7

EDEN

Ping.

I blink at the clock on my nightstand. It's just after two a.m.

Even though I should know better, I open the *Temptation* app anyway.

I won't respond, I tell myself. *I just want to know what he has to say.*

Devil: Happy birthday, beautiful.

My heart folds like a cheap lawn chair.

AngelBaby123: Fuck off.
Devil: You're mad at me.
AngelBaby123: Wow, you don't miss a thing.
Devil: Want me to kick his ass?
AngelBaby123: What I want is for you to stop hurting me.
Devil: I don't mean to.
AngelBaby123: And yet you keep doing it.
Devil: I didn't want to ignore you. I had some things to take care of.

AngelBaby123: This isn't about ignoring me. This is about what happened tonight.
Devil: Tell me what hurt you the most so I can kiss it better.
AngelBaby123: You can't this time. I'm not some little kid with a scraped knee.

I'm a girl with a permanent broken heart. Because I'm in love with a man I can never have.

Devil: I can if you let me. Give me your pain, Eden. Make me feel it so you don't have to anymore.
Devil: I promise it won't hurt so much once you do.

I wipe the tears dripping down my face with the back of my hand. This Cain always knows the right words to say.

But neither Cain knows how to prove it.

AngelBaby123: Don't say things you don't mean. And don't make promises you'll never keep.
AngelBaby123: And don't tell me to give you my pain because unlike you, I would never hurt the person I love.
Devil: I don't mean to hurt you.
AngelBaby123: Then why do you?
Devil: Because it's easier to hurt the person you love when they're not the person you should love. It's easier to push them away because your life would be so much better if you did.
AngelBaby123: Then why do you keep pulling me back?

Keep giving me hope.

Devil: Because I'm sick and selfish. I should let you go, but I don't want to lose you. I don't want to lose you because I don't want anyone else to have you. This thing between us is terrifying. It's ruining me.
AngelBaby123: So that makes it okay to ruin me?

The bottom of my screen says he's typing, but then it goes blank. Like he erased everything he wanted to say.

AngelBaby123: I guess I have my answer. Have a nice night, Mayor.
Devil: Don't hate me. I was only doing what I thought was right. The next two weeks will be the hardest of my life. So if I'm acting like an asshole to you, and I obviously am, it's only because I'm scared about the future.

I'm scared about the future too.

AngelBaby123: I'm tired. I'm gonna go back to sleep.
Devil: I don't want you going to bed upset with me. Can we start over?
AngelBaby123: How can we start over when we never began?
Devil: Don't give up on us. Let me make this right.
AngelBaby123: How?
Devil: I'm sending you a surprise soon.
AngelBaby123: What kind of surprise?
Devil: I'm giving you everything you ever wanted. All you have to do is take it.
AngelBaby123: What? How?

His username turns gray.

Chapter 8
CAIN

"Can you check on Eden for me? She still hasn't come downstairs."

Claudia raises one gray eyebrow. "I told you ten minutes ago that Eden said she wasn't feeling well."

"You did?" I look down at the paperwork on my desk. "Sorry, it's been one of those mornings."

"I imagine it has. Tonight's the big night."

When I stare at her blankly, she sighs and says, "The ball."

"Oh, right."

She looks in the direction of the staircase. "Poor thing is sick on her birthday."

Guilt settles over me. Eden's not sick…not physically anyway.

"Make sure someone checks on her while I'm gone for the day."

I don't want to ruin Eden's birthday by forcing her to see me… but I don't want her to be alone either.

Claudia glowers. "You don't have anything on the schedule other than the ball."

Claudia's advanced age works in her favor because if it was anyone else questioning my whereabouts, they'd be tossed from my office without so much as a severance check.

"I'm having lunch with Milton Bexley…and his daughter."

"Hmm."

I grab my suit jacket from the back of my chair and put it on. "Hmm? What's hmm?"

"Does Eden know yet?"

"Know what yet?"

"That you're dating Margaret Bexley?"

Claudia's more perceptive than I give her credit for. "Keep your voice down." I look around to make sure Eden isn't eavesdropping on our conversation. It wouldn't be the first time. "I haven't had a chance to tell her yet."

That's wrong, I've had plenty of chances to tell her over the last month…I just haven't.

I shoot Claudia a warning look. "I trust you'll keep this to yourself?"

"My gossiping days are long gone. Besides, it's better Eden hears this from you."

"I'll tell her when the time is right." I swipe my wallet and keys off the desk. "Did you order her present like I asked you to?"

She nods. "Should be delivered shortly."

"Perfect." I go to walk out, but my ears tune in to what's happening on the television.

"A young woman by the name of Jodie Gale is missing," the reporter says. "Her stepmother, Katrina Owens reports she was supposed to return home yesterday evening after work but never did. Our sources say Jodie's a junior gossip columnist at the Independent Chronicle."

I freeze when a photo of the young woman appears on the screen. "Fuck."

"Authorities are asking anyone who may have any information to contact them."

"Isn't she the reporter you threw out yesterday?" Claudia questions.

I glare at her. "No, she's the reporter I baked cookies for right before we roasted marshmallows and recited a few of our favorite Bible passages."

She opens her mouth, but I jam my finger into the wood of the desk. "Fix this shit, Claudia. Or enjoy living solely off your social security checks."

I'm out the door before she can argue.

Chapter 9

CAIN

Past...

"Sorry, man. I didn't want to be the one to tell you, but someone had to," my friend and sometimes rival in debate tells me. "I'd want to know if it were me."

I nod slowly, afraid to do more than that for fear it will only make the situation worse.

It's one thing to find out your girlfriend of a year and a half is cheating on you with the biggest asshole in school. It's another to have a mental breakdown in front of the entire student body over it.

Judging by the way everyone in the cafeteria is currently eyeballing me…I'm the last to know. Awesome.

I slap Corey's shoulder. "Thanks, man. Appreciate the heads up."

I keep my expression neutral as I wade through the cafeteria.

I'm not sure whether to confront her now or later. *Later*, I decide. Not only do I not know where she is, but I have no desire to catch her in the act.

"Wait," Corey yells and I stop walking.

"They're in the shed near the shop room," he informs me, louder than he needs to.

Make that now.

I'm sure a small part of him is enjoying this. He asked Katrina Owens—the cheater—to go to homecoming at the start of our junior year, but she turned him down and went with me instead.

We've been together ever since.

Until she started fucking Damien King behind my back.

It would almost be comical if it wasn't happening to me.

The two of us couldn't be more different from one another. So different I don't know much about him and I'm sure he can say the same about me.

What I do know about him isn't good, though. He doesn't run with a bad crowd…he is the bad crowd. His mother isn't in the picture—not sure why—but he lives with his father who's loaded. Not that being well off is an anomaly in this town, but his father is a callous businessman and most people in Black Hallows hate him. With good reason.

For instance—a few years back, our town was hit with a bad storm and a beloved ice cream shop was severely damaged. The owner, Mr. Manning—a nice man in his eighties didn't have the money to fix it. Naturally, the community came together and organized a huge fundraiser to help. However, a few days before it was supposed to take place, Mr. King stepped in and handed Mr. Manning a check. The old man was so grateful, he must not have realized what the paperwork he signed entailed.

A week later, Damien's father had it bulldozed to the ground and turned it into a gym.

To this day the man has never stepped foot inside of it. He just did it to piss everyone off.

And the apple doesn't fall far because most can say the same about Damien.

He pisses a lot of people off.

Like me. Right now.

Because I'm watching him nail my girlfriend against a wall in a shed.

I should probably stop them, but for some reason, all I can think about is how Katrina and I lost our virginities to each other ten months ago.

It would have been sooner if it were up to me, but Katrina said she wanted to wait. She claimed she was a good girl and wanted to make sure I was serious about her before we took it to the next level.

She doesn't look like such a good girl right now though.

Her legs are wrapped around his waist. Her fake nails are digging into his back. And brazen moans are spewing from her whore mouth while he fucks her so hard the shed vibrates.

No, she's not a good girl. Or rather…she was never this much of a good girl for me.

"Oh my God," Katrina squeals when she notices me.

Leaning against an oversized tool chest, I give her a tight smile. "Having fun?"

"Cain, I'm so—" She slaps Damien's shoulder. "Stop. My boyfriend's here."

"Hold on," Damien barks, his thrusts picking up speed. "You can have her back in a minute, bro. Just need to bust this nut first."

I stuff my hands in my pockets. "It's cool, *bro*. Take your time."

Take your time busting a nut inside my girlfriend while I stand here.

Katrina's eyes fill with tears. "I'm so…" Her voice trails off and her breathing accelerates.

I assume it's because she's so overcome with emotion and remorse for what she did.

That is until her head lolls back and she moans loud enough to wake the dead. "Oh, God. Don't stop."

Tilting my head to the side, I look down at where their bodies are joined…where Damien's hand is strumming her cunt like a banjo.

Evidently, fucking my girlfriend in front of me isn't good enough for him. He needs to pour salt in the wound by making sure I witness him getting her off in front of me too.

I grind my molars. The asshole is intentionally provoking me.

And it's working because my composure's akin to a rubber band about to snap.

Never let them see you sweat. My father's words of wisdom echo through the walls of my skull. *The key to surviving any scandal is to act like there isn't one.*

And let's not forget his latest. *Katrina seems a little slutty, son. Your future wife should be your accessory, not everyone else's.*

Turns out my father was right. I'm sure he'll love hearing me admit it when I go home.

"Finished yet?" I bite out through clenched teeth.

Thrust. "Just." *Thrust.* "One." *Thrust.* "Fuck. There we go." He shudders. "Yeah, baby, squeeze your snatch around me and milk it."

I want to kill him.

I watch in disgust as they disassemble themselves and put their clothes back on. Well, Katrina does.

The fucker barely puts his dick away before he's reaching for his cigarettes.

How any chick in their right mind would choose him over me is anyone's guess. Despite his bank account having more money than my own will ever see, he looks like trash. I'm not being facetious either. The dude actually looks like he smells bad. Then again, everything smells bad currently since I'm inhaling the musky scent of their post-coital bliss.

Narrowing my eyes, I continue my appraisal. His dark hair is cropped close, but thanks to the view I was afforded during the show, I know there are a few designs shaved into the back of his scalp.

As if that's not weird enough, smack center in the middle of his neck is a huge skull tattoo with flames expanding across his throat. His arms are also covered in a few skulls, along with a few *profound* statements like 'Trust No One.'

His body might be a little better than mine, I suppose. If you're into that sort of thing. We're both over six feet, but I'm lean and toned thanks to my years of running track. And he's…I guess someone's getting use out of the gym his father built after all.

I definitely have him beat in the facial area, though. Unlike him, I'm well-groomed and clean-cut. Unfortunately, the constant stubble on his face does little to dull his intense features. Downright *creepy* features if I'm being honest. Especially those icy blue eyes of his that chicks fawn over. They don't even look real. Fucker probably wears contacts.

Those unusual eyes aren't his most disturbing feature, though. It's what goes on behind them. The *look* he gives you. It's downright menacing. Almost like Satan himself is using him as a host to steal your soul.

Hell, maybe Katrina's not a two-timing tramp after all and this is the devil's work.

Or maybe, I need to stop procrastinating and kick her ass to the curb already.

Goddammit, this sucks. Despite my father's reservations, Katrina fit into my life perfectly. She knew my aspirations, knew what was expected of her, and cheating whore aside, would have been a good wife.

Her uncle is a congressman, so politics aren't a foreign concept to her or her family. Her parents aren't rich, but they are hardworking people. Something that would have made people support her, and in turn, support me. She came from good stock.

Not to mention—people enjoy a high school sweethearts love story when it comes to their politicians.

But there's no way I can stay with her given everyone knows she cheated on me with Damien King of all people.

She ruined everything. And now that the dust is starting to settle…it hurts. Losing her is like losing a block of wood you took the time to personally carve out in order to fit the part of your puzzle that needed to be filled.

A year and a half down the drain. Just like that.

God, I hate wasting my time. Especially when chances are she's just going to end up with some other aspiring politician who will profit from all the hard work I put into her.

"I'm so sorry, Cain," Katrina says, bringing me out of my thoughts.

I cross my arms over my chest. "Me too."

Her gaze darts around the room, looking everywhere else but at me. "It's just...you're always so busy all the time, and Damien—"

"Does nothing but fuck and smoke weed all day."

She blinks. "Well, yeah." She looks at him. "No offense."

He lights his cigarette. "None taken."

"It's just...I don't know. Everything between us seemed like it was on autopilot lately," Katrina continues. "We barely see one another because you're always so busy with student council and the debate team. And whenever we do hang out, it's always the same thing. We go to Fatty's, meet up with your friends, and then screw for five minutes in the back of your car until you drop me off at home."

Damien snorts.

I narrow my eyes at him before addressing Katrina. "First of all, it's not five minutes. It's *never* five minutes. Secondly, if you wanted to switch things up with our routine, you should have opened your mouth and said something."

"I did." Mascara streaks line her cheeks. "I told you last week and you ignored me."

"Last week I was filling out college applications. I was a little distracted."

Especially since my brother already found out he was accepted to Harvard. He's not only six minutes older than me, he also surpasses me on nearly everything that matters. Grades, sports, politics, looks...our father's approval.

She jerks her chin at Damien who's watching our exchange with a humorous expression on his face. "Well, that makes two of us." She buttons her cardigan. "I'm sorry, Cain but—"

"Wait," I interject because there's no way in hell I'm letting her fuck him in front of me and then turn right around and break up with me. People might be eavesdropping outside, and I won't let her make me look like a chump. "You've been fucking him since last week?"

She nods. He shrugs.

"We had sex yesterday," I remind her.

Damien looks unfazed by this information.

Katrina, however, looks guilty. "I'm—"

It's all I need.

"I don't want to hear your apology, Katrina." I roar loud enough she jumps. "Get the hell out of my face, you lying, cheating slut."

Her mouth drops open and she looks at Damien to defend her honor.

I tense, preparing for a fight. I don't want one, but it's pretty much unavoidable at this point thanks to my outburst.

To my surprise and bemusement, Damien remains silent as he takes another drag off his cigarette, appearing undeniably lackadaisical.

"All right, it's settled then. We're over." Straightening her spine, Katrina bats her eyelashes at Damien. "Call me later?"

Damien stares at her blankly. "I thought we were over?"

She looks about as confused as I feel. "Me and Cain are over, silly. Not us."

Damien looks positively disturbed. "I don't do girlfriends."

"Of course not," Katrina coos. "We've only been seeing each other for a week. It's too soon for that kind of talk."

"Fucking," Damien corrects. "I fucked you twice in the same week." He takes another long drag off his cigarette. "And only because I thought you already had a boyfriend and therefore *not* looking for one."

Well, this is awkward.

Katrina smiles nervously. "Can we not talk about this in front of Cain? I don't want to upset him more than he already is."

Jesus Christ. I suddenly feel like a child in the middle of a divorce.

"I'm not upset." *I'm a little upset.*

"Sorry to break it to you, sweetheart, but just because I shared the same cunt with your boyfriend, doesn't mean I share or inherit your relationship problems. The pussy is the only part I'm interested in." Damien stubs out his cigarette. "Unfortunately for you, yours is now past the acceptable expiration date."

Dammit, he not only screwed my girl, he also had a better breakup line.

Katrina understandably looks offended. "You're an asshole."

It's my turn to snort. Telling Damien King he's an asshole is like telling a deaf person they can't hear. *Utterly pointless.*

She grabs her purse. "The two of you can go to hell."

And she must be blind because I'm pretty sure I'm already here.

Damien laughs as she closes the shed door behind her.

"Something funny?"

He looks around. "You talking to me?"

"What are you, DeNiro? Of course, I'm talking to you. Who else is here—" The sound of clanking outside snags my attention. "What was that?"

He curses under his breath. "That was the sound of us getting fucked."

"I beg your pardon?"

He walks over to the door and pushes. "She locked us in here."

I walk over and try it myself. "Shit."

He rolls his creepy eyes. "Told you." He pulls out his cell phone from his pocket. "I'm gonna call someone who can get us out."

I look around. "We can probably get ourselves out. We are in the shop shed."

His tongue finds his cheek. "See a blowtorch around here?"

No. There's nothing but wood and basic hand tools. None of which do us any good since we're locked on the inside.

"Exactly." He brings the phone to his ear. "Yo, Bagels, it's D. Listen, I need a favor. I was fucking some bitch in the school shed, but shit went south, and she ended up locking me in here. My phone's about to die so don't call me back. Just get your ass to the shed with some bolt cutters." He's about to hang up but pauses. "And an eighth of that green lady. I'm good for it."

I glare at him. "Did you really just call your drug dealer for help?"

The last thing I need is to be discovered in the school shed with Cheech and Chong's long-lost brother and an eighth of weed four months before graduation.

My father will kill me.

He picks his cuticles. "If you're so concerned, call one of your own contacts and handle it yourself."

"I will." I feel around for my own phone but come up empty. "Shit."

"What's the matter, Mr. President? Find a hole in your polo?"

Annoyance skitters up my spine. "I left my phone in the cafeteria."

He throws his at me. "Knock yourself out."

I go to dial, but the phone screen goes black. "It's dead." Panic rivals my annoyance. "The only person who can help us now is a drug dealer named *Bagels* who's probably too stoned to remember his actual name let alone go on a rescue mission." I scowl. "How the hell my girlfriend cheated on me with someone like *you* is beyond me."

He lights another cigarette. "Bagels will come through. Dude can't say no to a sale. It's why I asked him to bring weed." He shrugs. "As for your chick…that's simple. I'm richer and I fuck better."

For a moment, I contemplate how to kill him and get away with it. Money is an extremely sore subject for me. Always has been. On the outside, my family looks like they do pretty well. And we would be…if it weren't for my father's bad habit of needing to be bigger and better than everyone else around him. His spending habits were easier when he still had my mom's trust money coming in, but he blew every cent of it—leaving nothing for me or my brother like she wanted.

In the last three years alone he's purchased two boats, four cars, a vacation home, and tons of other expensive things he'll never be able to pay off in his lifetime if he doesn't stop.

I can't even afford to go to college unless I get a full scholarship or take out a massive loan. Which of course, I'll be forced to do because my father won't allow me to be a disgrace and embarrass him.

And yet Damien can spend all his father's money on drugs and walk around intentionally looking like a bum.

"You're a scrub, Damien. You're not rich because you're intelligent and earned your money with your brain. You're nothing but a trust fund baby who will end up dying from a heroin overdose by thirty." I leer at him. "Don't worry, though. You'll leave behind three ex-wives who took you for whatever they could, and five kids who hate your guts because you're a shitty father." Amusement lines his face as I continue. "As for my bedroom skills, you don't know shit because I'm sure as hell not screwing you."

He blows a stream of smoke in my face. "A bit hypocritical, don't you think? You just told me my future and you don't even know me."

"You don't know me either, asshole."

"No, I don't." He stares at me for a long moment, pondering. "Well…I do know some things."

I hate myself for feeding into whatever bullshit game he's playing, but curiosity won't let it go. "Like what?"

I'm not sure what to make of the expression on his face. I can't tell if he hates me as much as I hate him, or if it amuses him he annoys me so much.

"I know your dad's a senator. I know you wear preppy shit like khakis and polos. I know you're on the debate team. I've heard you a few times—you're not bad…but you could be better." He takes a step in my direction. "I know your twin brother can be a dick…it's why people respect him more than you." He smirks. "I know Gerald Douglas was supposed to win the race against you for student body president, but you rigged the votes." He fixes my collar and winks. "I know your dad's credit card got declined at the country club the other day—because I fuck one of the waitresses and she couldn't stop laughing about it when I saw her later that night."

He inches closer and it's all I can do not to deck him. "And I know you never gave a shit about your little girlfriend—because if you did, you would have gone after her…instead, you're locked in here with me."

Tension locks my jaw when his lips hover over my ear. "You're just mad she played you and made you look like a sucker. Because Cain Carter can't be anything less than perfect, can he? He has to remain in complete control and be an angel at all times. He has to color inside the lines and stick to the script. Just like his daddy taught him." His voice drops to a whisper and the tiny hairs on the back of my neck stand on end. "We both know you don't hate me because I fucked your girlfriend…you hate me because I fucked her better and live my life the way you wish you had the guts to."

I open my mouth to respond, but the sound of something clanking outside catches my attention.

Damien, the fucker, chuckles under his breath. "That must be Bagels." He throws his cigarette on the ground and steps on it. "Catch you later." He starts walking toward the door but pauses. "If you ever want to stop being a pussy and have some fun, you know where to find me."

"Go fuck yourself."

His cruel, mocking laughter as he walks out of the shed has me thinking up ways to hurt him.

But it also has me wondering what it would be like to be Damien King for a day and live life the way he does.

To break all the rules and not give a fuck about the consequences.

Chapter 10
EDEN

"What is it?"

Claudia shrugs, appearing just as baffled by the two large boxes as I am. "I have no idea. It came addressed to the birthday girl."

I eye her skeptically. I know for a fact the woman had a hand in all the gifts I've received from Cain this year.

I look at the diamond tennis bracelet on my wrist. It's thin, delicate, and perfect. One of the best birthday presents I've ever received. Claudia might have hideous taste in clothing, but her eye for jewelry is on point.

"Oh, it came with a note." She makes a face as she hands me a manila envelope. "Feels like there's something else in there too."

This is getting stranger and stranger by the second.

I go to reach for it but pause, trying to figure out a polite way to tell her to leave. Cain said he was sending me a surprise soon, and if this is it, I don't want to open it in front of her.

Luckily, I don't have to because Claudia places the envelope on the bed beside me and says, "I'll give you some privacy."

I pick it up, but then I notice one of the boxes—the biggest of the two—has *Open me first* scrawled on it.

I bite the inside of my cheek as I take the top off the box and wade through the mountains of tissue paper. I don't want to smile since I'm still sad and angry with Cain…but I can't help myself.

Until I see what's inside.

Why in the world would Cain send me a dress? Especially one as extravagant as this?

Taking it out, I hold it up and examine it. It's completely sleeveless, and the bodice is black and form-fitting—highlighting the mermaid shape of the dress. Little red jewels run along the sweetheart neckline, giving it an elegant vibe. That alone is enough to make me fall in love, but my favorite part of the dress is the lower half. A dangerous slit mid-thigh leads to a floor-length gown made of sheer black tulle fabric edged with red ribbon.

It's gorgeous and sexy. But far too fancy for my usual movie nights.

My heart drops when I uncover a pair of black strappy shoes under another layer of tissue paper and put the pieces together.

He knows I can't go there tonight. I don't know why he bothered going through the trouble of doing all this in the first place. All it does is remind me how much of a freak I am.

I go to open the second box next, hoping to find a note saying not to worry about the party because we'll have our own masquerade ball at home—but it instructs me to open the envelope first, so I do.

To say I'm confused would be an understatement because when I look inside all I see is a tiny scrap of black lace and a single string of pearls.

I swallow hard when I realize it's a *G-string* made of pearls…along with a note.

Wear these for me tonight.

P.S: Don't chicken out. Open the last box.

. . .

My heart rate accelerates. It's such a bittersweet feeling wanting something so much…but knowing you can never have it because your own mind won't let you.

I love Cain, but I'm not strong like he is. I can't walk into a room full of people who hate my existence. I can't stand there and smile while they all whisper horrible and untrue things about me. I'll run out in tears and embarrass myself even more.

My stomach churns with an evil lurch when I take the top off the last box and see a beautiful masquerade mask that matches my dress, along with another note.

We all hide behind a mask, Eden.

Show them yours and I'll take off mine tonight.

Tears prickle my eyes because he's not playing fair. He knows I'm not strong enough to do this.

Wiping my cheeks, I grab my phone and click open the *Temptation* app.

AngelBaby123: This isn't fair.
AngelBaby123: I can't do this.
Devil: Yes, you can.
AngelBaby123: I can't turn my illness on and off like a lightbulb. It doesn't work like that.
Devil: What's your worst fear?
AngelBaby123: What?
Devil: What scares you the most about going to the party?
AngelBaby123: The people. I'm afraid they'll all laugh and say cruel things because of who I am. What they *think* I am…thanks to the rumors.
Devil: What if you weren't Eden tonight?

AngelBaby123: A fancy dress and a mask doesn't change who I am. Everybody will know.
Devil: Put the mask on.
AngelBaby123: This is stupid.

Despite myself, I do what he says anyway.

AngelBaby123: It's on.
Devil: Good girl. Now look in the mirror.

I pad over to my vanity and sit.

AngelBaby123: Okay.
Devil: What do you see? Not what you think you see, but what you actually see staring back at you?
AngelBaby123: A girl with a mask on her face.
Devil: Tell me who she is.
AngelBaby123: Is this a trick question?
Devil: No. Who is the girl you're looking at? Who do you want her to be tonight?
AngelBaby123: I'm not sure I know how to answer that.
Devil: Yes, you do.

I close my eyes. I don't need to look in the mirror to see everything I wish I was. It's already burned into my heart.

AngelBaby123: I want her to be brave.
Devil: She's very brave. She knows what she wants and she's not afraid to go after it.
AngelBaby123: I want her to be beautiful.
Devil: She's the most beautiful woman in a room.
AngelBaby123: I want her to be yours.
Devil: Then meet me tonight. I'll send a driver to pick you up in a few hours.

Before I can protest, his username turns gray.

Chapter 11
CAIN

Past...

"Are you going to the spring fling?" Julia Brown asks, her voice barely above a whisper.

Peeling my gaze away from the board full of trigonometry questions, I look at her. "I don't know. Haven't really thought about it."

The pen she's chewing on like a rabid animal nearly snaps. "Gosh, I'm so dumb."

Julia's a weird girl.

However, she's also a smart girl—her SAT scores were off the charts. And now that I'm looking at her for more than a second, I realize she's kind of pretty. Flat chested and a little chubby…but cute. And she's without a doubt someone my father would approve of as long as I keep those pens far away.

Too bad I'm not even remotely attracted to her.

Which means she's ideal for me. Way better than Katrina who had a face and body that appealed to me and my cock.

Releasing a sigh, I mull over the idea of dating Julia.

I'm not proud of myself for categorizing girls based on what they can do for me, but it's been instilled in me since I was a kid. My father told me early on that I had a choice to make. If I pursued politics, I'd have to marry a girl who was good for me on paper but had no romantic or sexual feelings for. If not—I could be a dentist who goes home to the woman he loves with all his heart and soul night after night.

Because I couldn't have both.

Emotions—especially love—have no place in politics.

"You're not dumb." I give Julia a smile. I might not be attracted to her, but she's officially on my list of potential options. "Thanks for reminding me about the dance."

She blushes. "No problem. I wasn't sure if you were going or not because of the whole…you know. You and Katrina." She lowers her voice. "For what it's worth, I always thought you could do way better than her."

I give her a tight nod.

Katrina and I have been broken up for a little over a week now. She's called me twice since then, but I have nothing to say to her. Unlike the rest of my classmates who are still gossiping about her cheating on me with Damien.

Granted, the chatter about us isn't as bad as it was when it was fresh. But still…they're talking.

Maybe going to this stupid dance with Julia will prove to everyone I've moved on and they should too.

I lean over. "When is it again?"

She nearly chokes on her pen. "Next Friday at eight. In the school gymnasium." She frantically jots something down on a sheet of paper and hands it to me. "Here, I wrote the date down so you won't forget." She comes up for air. "The theme is masquerade."

I inwardly groan. Why is this town obsessed with masquerade parties? It's bad enough we have one every year at the old Vanderbilt castle for Halloween. Is it really necessary for them to turn our senior spring fling into one, too?

I take the paper from her and tuck it away. "Thanks." I start to ask her if she has a date, but the bell cuts me off.

Julia stands, and I follow suit as students fly out of the classroom for dismissal. Not me, though because I'm staying after school to run a student council meeting.

She chews on her pen coyly, which might be cute if it didn't look like a German Shepard already got to it. "So, does this mean you're gonna go?"

I stuff my trig book under my arm. "Yeah, sounds fun. Plus, I'm expected to attend all school functions."

"Right, duh." She taps her head. "You are our president."

My grin is smug. "That I am."

"And you're *so* good at it. God, you're like the best President ever. Even better than the real one."

Hmm. Maybe dating her won't be so bad after all. She's easy on my ego, that's for sure.

I rub the back of my neck, trying my best to look humble. "You're sweet. But I'm just a regular guy trying to do what's best for everyone. I'm no one special."

She eats it up. "And that right there is what makes you even more amazing. You're so kind and nice. But you're also commanding and powerfu—"

"Where the fuck is my phone, Carter?" Damien booms from the classroom door.

Shit.

"Sorry, man. Forgot it again. I'll bring it tomorrow."

"You said that yesterday." He takes a step closer. "And the day before that." Another step. "And the day before that." Another step. "And the—"

"Day before that," I finish for him. "I get the picture. Look, I'm sorry to inform you, but my life doesn't revolve around you. I'm a busy man and bringing you your phone isn't on my list of priorities."

Julia's gaze ping-pongs between us cautiously. "Should I go?"

"No," I say at the same time Damien hisses, "Yes."

Julia looks like a deer caught in headlights and it only gets worse when Damien turns his creepy eyes on her.

Instantly, she swipes her purse off her desk, nearly dropping the stack of books she's holding.

"Let me know about the dance, Cain," she squeaks as she hustles to the door. "I wrote my number down on the paper."

"Was that really necessary?"

His lips twitch. "Not my fault little Miss Chewy is skittish." His expression turns serious. "What are you doing with my phone?"

"I'm not doing anything with your phone," I snap, making a mental note to cover my tracks tonight before I return it. "I have my own phone. What in the world would I want with yours?"

He gets uncomfortably close to my face. "You have until tomorrow to return it. Or else."

"Or else what?"

"Is there a problem here?" Mr. Turner questions, popping his head inside the classroom.

Damien fixes my collar. "No. Just asking my boy Cain here for some study tips."

Mr. Turner doesn't look like he's buying it for a second. "Considering you haven't turned in homework for me in two years, I find that hard to believe." He looks at me. "You okay, Cain?"

"Yeah." I hike my bookbag up my shoulder. "I borrowed a textbook from Damien last week and forgot to return it. We were just figuring out our schedules and making arrangements."

Damien nods. "Yup." He slaps my shoulder so hard I almost wince. "I have Mrs. Miller for eighth period tomorrow. Make sure you bring it to me by then, pal."

With that, he walks out with Mr. Turner right on his heels.

A moment later the phone in my pocket vibrates. I peer around the classroom to make sure it's empty before I take it out.

Kristy: You're so dirty, Damien.

Another text immediately follows that one.

Kristy: My body is craving you. I need you to fuck me like your life depends on it after classes end tomorrow.

I do another look around before I type out my response.

Damien: Tell me everything you want me to do to that hot little cunt of yours and I'll consider it.

Chapter 12
EDEN

AngelBaby123: I don't think I can do this.

His username is gray, and I know he probably won't see my message until after the party.

And I'll have lost my one and only chance.

I'm not stupid. I know this is Cain's way of testing me again. He probably wants to make sure I can handle being out of my comfort zone by doing the one thing that scares me the most. He wants to see if I have what it takes to make our relationship work because there are so many obstacles in our way.

Exhaling sharply, I clutch my chest. *God, I'm so nervous.* My heart is beating so hard it hurts.

"Everything okay, miss?" the driver questions.

No, everything is not okay. Cain's ignoring me and I'll be arriving at the Vanderbilt castle in ten minutes.

I love him.

From the soles of my shoes to the top of my head, I'm in love with Cain Carter.

And if I want everything he's willing to give me…everything I've dreamed of since the first time he looked at me and stole my heart, I have no choice but to walk inside that party.

I can do this.

I can do this for him.

I can do this for us.

"I'm fine," I tell the driver. "But would you mind rolling down the window? It's a little hot in this get-up."

He nods. "Not a problem, miss."

Closing my eyes, I inhale in the fresh air. When my nerves threaten to skyrocket again, I force myself to take a few calming breaths.

I can be anyone I want tonight, I remind myself. Just like Cain said.

And tonight? I'm no longer the Eden who's damaged and scared of her own shadow.

Tonight, this Eden is confident, sexy, and beautiful.

Tonight, this Eden is brave.

Tonight, I'm no longer the girl with a broken heart.

I'm the girl who takes what she wants.

Chapter 13
CAIN

Past...

It's weird mourning a life that doesn't belong to you. Not that I'm proud of what I've done. Pretending to be someone you're not is wrong.

No matter how fun it can be.

Kristy: I'm naked.
Kristy: Waiting for you to come in here so you can tie me up and ram that fat dick of yours in my ass.

I damn near whimper as I read her texts. I want to respond… no, fuck that. I want to find her and shove my fat dick in her ass—but it's the end of the day and I have to return Damien's phone.

Not that it would matter if I didn't. I'm pretty sure Kristy—whoever she is—would call the cops if I showed up instead of Damien.

My fingers itch to respond, but I shove them in my pocket.

Late last night I went through Damien's phone and erased all the texts I sent to Kristy and a few other chicks he talks to.

The last text Kristy sent is a good place for them to rekindle their relationship, though so I won't delete it.

Christ, I hate him. The guy has it all.

My mood is grim as I continue walking down the hall to Mrs. Miller's classroom. I'm ten minutes late, but considering Damien hasn't gone on a search mission to find me, that's a good sign.

Or maybe not, seeing as the classroom's empty when I arrive.

With a sigh, I walk over to one of the lab tables in the front. Mrs. Miller is the new science teacher at Black Hallows. She's also hot as hell. Every guy in my senior class—even the dumb ones—managed to get a B+ or higher in biology this year. I think it's safe to say Black Hallows High will keep her on board.

It's a shame I can't re-take her class after I graduate. It might be worth another year of this crap to see her killer legs in those short skirts she wears. Her husband—the assistant football coach—is one lucky son of a bitch.

I place Damien's phone on the desk—because I have better things to do with my life than wait for him to show up—and turn to leave.

I'm halfway to the door when I hear someone moan. Well, not just anyone. A female.

I should mind my business, but my curiosity gets the best of me when I realize it's coming from the lab closet behind the teacher's desk.

Wandering over, I look through the small glass window of the closet door…and nearly pass out.

Because there's Mrs. Miller…getting pounded in her tight little ass by none other than Damien King.

"Grab your ankles, Mrs. Miller," Damien instructs, and fuck me because this shit is better than porn. Especially when it's not your girlfriend he's screwing.

Adjusting my backpack on my shoulder, I cup my hand over the glass so I can get a better look.

"I told you to call me Kristy," Mrs. Miller rasps as she grabs her ankles.

I freeze, hoping I'm hearing things.

"If you let me smear my cum all over your asshole and lick my fingers clean, I'll call you whatever you want."

Fucking hell. I should leave.

"Deal."

My legs don't seem to get the signal…because both my brain and dick are too busy watching Damien spread Mrs. Miller's ass cheeks while he continues ramming his dick inside her sphincter.

Jesus. I spent a year and a half with Katrina and she never let me see that part of her. The craziest thing we ever did was sixty-nine…and that was for special occasions. Yet here Damien is, hammering the ass of the hottest teacher I've ever seen in my life while she asks him to call her by her first name.

What the hell does he have that I don't?

Whatever it is must be good, because a moment later, he shoots his load all over her plump behind and she does exactly what she promised.

My balls twitch as I watch her lick the cum off his fingers…and they downright ache when she gets on her knees and cleans his dick next.

I spin around, intending to leave thanks to my now raging hard-on. I'm almost to the door when I pass his phone on the desk I left it on. I'm in a Catch-22 because I don't want Damien to know I was here while he was having sex with Mrs. Miller…but I also don't want to deal with him anymore.

Sadly, my split-second of hesitation costs me because I hear the closet door open.

Like a kid caught with his hand inside the cookie jar, I go into panic mode and start running for the door. Unfortunately, I fail to take the chairs and tables in my way into consideration. Desperate, I make a sharp left, trying to find a clear path to the exit.

"Oh my God," Mrs. Miller—Kristy—shrieks.

I feel like a wild animal about to be caged.

"I didn't see anything," I yell, which is hands down the stupidest thing to say in this situation.

"He…he…" Mrs. Miller stammers when Damien walks out behind her. "Cain's here."

Damien, as usual, remains unfazed. "Told you to cover the window on the door."

"I can't cover the window," she whisper-shouts. "It's against school policy."

Damien shrugs. "So is screwing a student."

She glares at him. "I have no clue what you're talking about. You stayed after for extra credit. I was simply helping you find the materials you needed to get your project done."

I'll say.

She gives me a saccharine smile. "I assure you there's nothing inappropriate going on."

Damien rolls his eyes. "Cain's not dumb. The worst thing to do when someone has leverage against you is act like they're stupid or delusional. It only pisses them off."

He's not wrong. Although I wouldn't mind rewinding the last ten minutes.

With the exception of seeing Mrs. Miller's ass.

Blowing out a breath, she clutches her chest. "You're right." She looks at me. "Cain, please don't—"

"Is that my phone?" Damien moseys over to the desk and picks it up. "About time."

Mrs. Miller blinks. "Cain had your phone?"

Oh fuck. "No."

"Yeah—" Damien's creepy eyes flick to mine. "What's your deal, Carter?"

Shit.

I can see the wheels turning in Mrs. Miller's head, but before I can explain, she blurts out, "How long did he have it?"

Much like Mrs. Miller was in that closet, I'm screwed. Not only will Damien pound my face in for pretending to be him, but these things have a way of coming back to bite you in the ass when you least expect it.

Being cautious about my behavior is something my father has

always instilled in me. The worst thing in the world would be finally becoming a senator, or my ultimate goal—President—down the road and having my lewd and vulgar texts to a teacher come to light.

People get off on making those with power suffer for their sins. No matter how many they've committed themselves. *Hypocrisy at its finest.*

It's why I always play by the rules. It's not just my present I have to think about…it's my future. *Always my future.*

Damien's mouth curves into a cruel smirk and I know he's about to fuck me as hard as he fucked our biology teacher. "A little over a week." His lips twitch as he turns to her. "Why?"

Her cheeks take on a tomato color and it's enough for Damien to put two and two together. "I *knew* it." To my surprise, he laughs. "Damn, Cain. Didn't think you had it in you." He presses a few buttons on his phone and clicks his teeth. "You even got rid of the evidence like a good little politician."

I swallow, and it feels like nails going down. I need to get the hell out of this room. "Look, Mrs. Miller, your secret is safe with me—"

"No." Damien's finger zags between us. "This isn't right."

Needless to say, I'm confused. "I don't follow."

He cracks his knuckles and circles us slowly, like a vulture looming over its prey. "The way I see it, there's only one way to fix this." He points to himself. "I mean, I'm not the one who has anything to lose from what transpired today. Unlike Mrs. Miller, I'm just an innocent bystander." He comes to a stop in front of her. "If I were in your position, I'd figure out a way to gain Cain's trust." He slides his hand up her arm and looks at me. "She's a good teacher, Cain. She comes here early, stays late. Really goes the extra mile for us." His hand travels to her ass. "She works her students hard, and she's always available when you need a little help." He licks his fingers and slips his hand under her skirt. "I'm sure she'd be more than happy to help you study." I watch his arm move back and forth, my mind conjuring up all sorts of dirty images of what he's doing to her under there. "Isn't that right, Kristy."

Mrs. Miller nods. "Of course." Her chest heaves and she bites her lower lip. "Just tell me the area you want help with."

I'm pretty sure I stop breathing. I thought keeping Damien's phone and pretending to be him was wrong, but it has nothing on watching him finger fuck Mrs. Miller and manipulate her into giving me sexual favors.

And deep down—okay, maybe not that deep—I'd love to take her up on her offer.

But, my conscience won't let me. I'm not perfect, but for the most part, I consider myself to be a decent human being.

Unlike most politicians, I chose politics for the right reasons. I honestly believe I can make a positive difference in the world.

And unlike Damien—my selfish wants and desires don't trump my ethics and morals.

"That won't be necessary, Mrs. Miller." I hold up my hands. "Damien's eighteen. Therefore, you're both consenting adults. What you do in private is none of my business and you certainly don't owe me anything for my silence."

I'm not sure what to think of the look Mrs. Miller and Damien exchange.

"It's really not a problem." Her eyes become hooded and she looks at my crotch. "Just tell me what you'd like to focus on and I'll be happy to help you."

I wonder if something in the lab exploded and I'm hallucinating.

That would explain why I'm about to turn her down. "I appreciate the offer, but—"

"He'd like a blow job," Damien chimes in. "Seeing you naked got him harder than a rock and now the poor guy has blue balls. You should do something to relieve him."

"Is that what you want?" Mrs. Miller questions. "Do you want me to take care of you? Perhaps do that thing you talked about last night."

My dick strains against my zipper, liking that very much.

I open my mouth to decline again, but no sound comes out. All I can think about is her lips wrapped around me. Maybe I can convince her to let me stick it where Damien did and make her clean me up too after we're done.

As if sensing my internal struggle, Damien leans over and whispers, "You'll regret it if you don't. She's got a mouth like a Hoover."

My heart pounds in my chest when he removes his hand from underneath her skirt and shoves his fingers into her mouth so she can demonstrate her skills.

Christ, I'm so turned on it's almost painful. One wrong move and I'm liable to bust a nut in my pants.

Surely putting my morals on hold so a smoking hot teacher can suck me off is the better way to end this ordeal.

"The only way to stop temptation is to give into it," Damien goads as he undoes the first two buttons on her blouse, giving me a peek at her lacy white bra. "Stop being a pussy and live a little."

I'd love to live life on the edge like Damien does, but unlike him, I have a future to worry about.

And a conscience that won't stop gnawing at me.

As if he knows how close I am to cracking, he takes a step in my direction. "No one has to know." His hand goes to my fly and he tugs my zipper down. "It will be our little secret."

Before I have time to react to the intrusion, he walks away. "Step off your moral high horse and stick your cock in her mouth."

As if on cue, Mrs. Miller drops to her knees. Mine turn to jelly.

I look at Damien who's now standing in front of the closed classroom door. "You're just gonna stand there and watch?"

He smirks. "Someone's gotta stand guard and make sure no one walks in while she's blowing you." He brings the apple he must have snatched off Mrs. Miller's desk to his lips and takes a bite. "Don't worry, I brought refreshments."

It's official. Damien King is the proverbial devil on my shoulder.

And God help me because I'm starting to listen to him.

"Take it out," Damien orders.

I glare at him. "She doesn't have to do anything she doesn't want to."

I look down at her. "You don't have to do—" White hot pleasure plows through me like a freight train when she takes me into her mouth. "Jesus fucking Christ, Mrs. Miller."

Damien laughs low and deep. "Told you she was good."

She's more than good, she's the goddamn goddess of giving head.

My enjoyment is short lived though, because my balls start tingling and I know this is going to be over way sooner than I want it to be.

I force myself to think of something…*anything* to hold off, but it's not working.

Especially when she speeds up her movements.

"Bet you wish you gave in sooner, huh?" Damien taunts.

My teeth clack with annoyance. "Will you shut the fuck up."

The only thing worse than coming before you want to…is having another guy witness it.

There's only one way to save my reputation and that's to go out with a bang.

I tug Mrs. Miller's hair until her head falls back and my dick pops out of her mouth.

"Open."

Aiming to please, she tries to put me in her mouth once more, but I tug her hair again. Much harder this time. "Did I tell you to suck it?"

Shaking her head, she looks at Damien.

Jealousy courses through my veins. I don't want her looking at Damien while my cock is in front of her face.

Before I can talk myself out of it, I wind her hair in my fist and slap her cheek with my dick. "Don't look at him."

It's such a vile, cruel thing to do. But it gets my point across… and fuck if it doesn't spark a hellfire of lust inside of me.

Competing with Damien is an intoxicating, dangerous mixture.

I stroke my pulsing dick. "You gonna be a good girl? Or do I have to slap that pretty face of yours with this again?"

Her eyes light up like Christmas trees. "I'll be anything you want me to be."

"Well, shit," Damien utters. "This just got interesting."

I jerk it faster, tuning him out. "Take out your tits."

The second she does, I shoot my load in thick, stringy ropes all over her mouth, face, and glorious tits. It makes me drunk with primal satisfaction. Like I've marked my territory in front of my rival.

Only, Damien's not the enemy.

He's more like a puppet master…pulling everyone's strings to get them to perform for his own enjoyment.

There's something oddly fascinating about it. It's as if you get to step outside yourself temporarily and walk into his world.

Mrs. Miller stands, and Damien tosses her a roll of paper towels. "You might want to clean up before you go home to your husband."

It's like he dumped a vat of ice water over my head. Not only did I slap my teacher's face with my prick and come all over her. I inadvertently helped her cheat on her husband.

I go to leave, but he drapes one arm around my shoulder and the other around Mrs. Miller's. "The three of us are going to have so much fun."

Mrs. Miller giggles, but I remove his arm and step away. "This was a one-time thing for me."

"Bullshit." He grins. "You enjoyed it too much to stop now."

He's right. It's addicting.

But trying a drug once doesn't make you an addict.

"I have to go. I'm late for a student council meeting."

I'm halfway down the empty hallway when I hear footsteps approaching behind me. I don't even have to turn around to know who it is.

"I'm disappointed in you, Mr. President."

"Fuck off, Damien."

"I'm good, thanks. Already cleaned my pipes in the science room storage closet."

"Yeah, and I bet you can't wait to tell everyone about it and ruin her life when she least expects it. Can you?"

Quicker than I can blink, he slams me against a locker. "Is that what your problem is? You think I'm some kind of snitch?"

"No." I bare my teeth. "I think you're a manipulative asshole who uses people for sport."

I'm not sure where this venom is coming from, all I know is it feels good to not hold back. I'm tired of keeping all my feelings—good and bad—hidden under my good boy exterior.

Those creepy blue eyes darken. "It's not using people if they like it."

He has a point. *Kind of.* "Enjoying something doesn't make it right."

"Aren't you sick of playing by the rules all the time?"

I'm so sick I could keel over. But I know what I want…and I know what path I need to take to get there.

Hanging around Damien and screwing hot married teachers, isn't it.

I need to keep my hands clean and my focus razor sharp.

"Do you know what you want to be when you grow up?"

Amusement lines his face. "Wow, you get one blow job from a teacher and you go all after-school special on me."

"I'm being serious. Do you know what you want to do with your life?"

"I'm not sure. Investing, maybe?" He shrugs. "Haven't really thought about it much."

That doesn't surprise me. We're two totally different people. Like oil and water, we don't mix.

"I've known what I wanted to be since I was five."

A scoffing noise escapes him. "I know, man. Everyone around here knows you want to follow in your daddy's footsteps and run for office."

"I'd want to run even if he wasn't my dad." I start walking and he follows. "It might sound stupid to some, but it feels right to me. It's my calling."

I expect him to laugh, but he doesn't. "Then you should follow it." We wander out to the parking lot and he lights a cigarette. "I don't see how having some fun and screwing a few girls is a crime."

"You know just as much as I do that people are inherently selfish. They'll throw anyone under the bus for payback, personal gain, or because something better comes along. I can't trust what I do now won't come back to bite me later on."

He takes a long drag off his cigarette. "For what it's worth, I'd never let any chick we mess with do that to you." He pulls out his phone and hands it to me. "Bros over hoes. Let's just call this one yours."

I blink, not understanding. "But it's your phone."

"It hasn't been mine for over a week." When I raise a brow, he pulls out another phone. "This one's mine."

I feel like I'm in the twilight zone. None of this shit makes any sense. "Why would you be okay with people thinking I'm you?"

He drops his cigarette and steps on it. "So you can be *you* without having to suffer the consequences. Every text you send to Mrs. Miller and whoever else is through my phone number. No one will be able to trace it back to you. Therefore, you don't have to worry about your past coming back to haunt you."

His statement only confuses me more. "Why would you do that?"

"I'm not really sure. Maybe I'm in the mood for a friend."

"You don't have friends."

"Exactly."

"Okay, let's say I went along with…whatever this is. How do I know I can trust you?"

"You don't."

I hand him back his phone. "Thanks for the offer, it's tempting, but I'm gonna pass."

"Why?"

"Are you dense? You just said it yourself. I can't trust you. Why in the world would I open myself up to that potential pitfall? There are plenty of girls my own age I can hook up with without all the bullshit yours bring."

"You're right." He stops walking when we reach my car. "There are plenty of sweet, wholesome girls who would give their left tit to suck your right nut…but you and I both know it's not the same. People like us need more than that. Their idea of a thrill is jerking their boyfriends off in a movie theater. Not the same shit we're into."

"You don't know what kind of shit I'm into."

"That's where you're wrong." He shoves me against my car. "I saw you in that classroom, brother. You're like a goddamn bomb ready to explode. And if you don't relieve some of that pent-up tension inside you, sooner or later you're going to detonate." He punches the side of my car. "Boom."

"No offense, but you're fucking crazy. I don't know what you think you know about me, but whatever it is, I guarantee you it's wrong. I'm fine, Damien. Unlike you, I'm *normal.*" I open my car door. "Go find someone else who wants to ride shotgun to your twisted shit."

White-hot pain sears through my body when he grabs my neck. "You have a bruise the size of Texas on your back, dude."

He releases me, but I stay put, too afraid to move or speak.

"And before you accuse me of stalking you, I have gym eighth period. I'm guessing you have gym seventh because you were still in the locker room changing when I arrived."

Finally, I find my voice. "I think you're mistaken."

He snorts. "About the line of bruises spanning from your neck to your ass…or the fact that your daddy is responsible for putting them there?"

In two fluid movements, my hand is wrapped around his throat. "You don't know what the hell you're talking about." I tighten my hold, watching his face change colors. "I fell down the stairs last week."

It's a lie and he knows it. But admitting your dad is still beating the shit out of you when you're about to graduate high school isn't something a man does.

Neither is disclosing the fact that your own brother picked up his bad habits. What started out as a regular argument last week ended with my brother taking a chair to my back.

Which of course led to my father taking off his belt while I was too weak to defend myself—because according to him, I must have provoked his favorite twin.

My family has problems…every family does. However, my family problems are *my* business, not his.

Despite his red face, Damien doesn't struggle. Instead, his blue eyes blaze, challenging me. Like he wants to see how far I'll go.

He coughs when I release him. "Like I said…boom."

"I thought you said you had Mrs. Miller for eighth period?" I yell when he stalks off.

Between the phone and his fixation on my personal life, I can't help but feel like he intentionally set me up to walk in there.

And if he'd go that far, there's no telling what else he would do if I agreed to this strange friendship.

He turns, arms wide. "Thought you said you had a student council meeting today?" He flips me the bird when I stay silent, his expression growing sinister. "Looks like we're both liars."

Chapter 14
CAIN

"I've arranged for the local newspaper to come by this week and do a story on the engagement," Milton Bexley informs me, his eyes zipping around the room. "Where is that goddamn waitress with the shish kabobs? Swear this event goes farther downhill every year."

"You already finished your second plate of hors-d'oeuvres, Daddy. The doctor said you need to watch your diet and cholesterol," Margaret scolds, nudging him with the stick of her purple masquerade mask.

A waitress appears at his side a moment later. "Would you like more?"

"Yes." I down the rest of my whiskey and place the empty glass on her tray. "Make it a double."

Milton nods. "Me too."

"Right away, sir," the waitress says at the same time Margaret hisses, "Daddy."

"Don't start," Milton grumbles. "Can't you see we're both celebrating the big news?"

He might be celebrating. I'm grieving.

The plan was to announce our engagement a few months *after* the election. However, Milton thinks doing it beforehand will encourage people to vote for me. According to several news sources, I'm starting to dip in the polls. It's not enough to make me panic since I'm still ahead…but downward slopes are never a good thing.

People are starting to doubt me and my capabilities.

Which is why I didn't put up much of a protest when what was supposed to be a business lunch turned into picking out engagement rings.

But right now? I'm having second thoughts about everything.

"Are you sure an engagement right before the election won't backfire? I don't want potential voters concerned about my focus shifting to my fiancée and the upcoming wedding instead of where it should be."

Margaret huffs, clearly offended.

Tough shit. It's what she signed up for.

"Personally, I'm more concerned about how your stepdaughter will handle the news." She takes a dainty sip of her champagne. "I used to volunteer at the local psychiatric hospital. Let's just say girls with her *issues* can be very co-dependent. It's going to be quite an adjustment period for her when she moves out."

"Eden isn't moving out." I scan the ballroom for the waitress because I could use that second drink *now*. "And she's not psychotic. She just has a few issues she needs to work on."

"Don't we all," Milton drawls.

"Sorry, but I'm not comfortable with my husband living under the same roof with someone like her." The mask shielding her face does little to hide her annoyance. "I don't know any woman who would be."

If I don't put my foot down about Eden now, she'll keep pushing the issue. "I'm not kicking Eden out of her mother's house."

"That's fine. Leave her there and we'll move into our own."

"I don't feel right leaving her all alone."

"Why not? It's not like she's your actual daughter."

"It's non-negotiable."

Margaret crosses her arms. "Daddy."

Milton sighs. "Cain, Margaret has a point. You don't want to give people something to talk about."

I was hoping the three of us living as one happy family would prove to everyone for once and all that Eden isn't a homewrecker and stop all the gossip.

As if sensing the tension brewing in our circle, the waitress delivers our drinks.

I take a large swig of mine before I speak. "She doesn't have any other family. Her mother only passed away a year ago. I wouldn't feel right leaving her on her own so soon."

"Shish kabob," Milton reminds the waitress and she runs off.

Margaret rolls her eyes. "Please, she's hardly a child. Besides, it's not like you'll be leaving town. You can call and check in with her from time to time." Her lips form a tight line. "Most girls her age are heading off to college and living on their own."

Milton swipes a shish kabob off a nearby waitress's tray. "Come to think of it, that's not a bad idea."

I raise a brow. "What's not a bad idea?"

"Sending the girl away to college. If you're so worried about her well-being, then ensuring she receives a proper education is the best thing you can do for her and her future."

"Daddy's right." Margaret croons. "Education is very important. Who knows? She could become the next great biophysicist and find a cure for cancer."

Milton chuckles. "Let's not get ahead of ourselves."

Despite the knot forming in my stomach, I know it's the best solution for all involved. Eden needs to spread her wings…and I need to forget about her and keep my focus where it should be.

She'll never go for it, though.

I clear my throat. "She's already enrolled in a few online courses."

Margaret waves a hand. "That's not a problem, she can transfer her credits."

I smile because people are starting to look at us. "Leaving Black Hallows isn't an option for Eden at this juncture."

Milton picks his teeth with a kabob stick. "Why not?"

"Because she doesn't leave the house," Margaret snaps. "What has it been, Cain? Three, four years now?"

My hands itch with the urge to put them over her mouth. She's starting to remind me of Karen and I refuse to marry another woman who makes me miserable.

I push my mask up and loosen my bowtie, hoping it will help me breathe easier.

It doesn't. I feel like the walls are closing in on me.

Milton must sense my irritation and impending cold feet because he says, "Enough about the girl, Margaret."

"But, Daddy—"

"This pushy behavior is why you're almost thirty and single."

Her lower lip trembles. "I'm assertive. There's nothing wrong with that."

"You nag," Milton snaps. "Men don't like it."

Blinking back tears, she inhales sharply. "I'm sorry, Cain. This was the wrong time and place to bring it up." She holds the mask over her face. "It is a party after all."

Milton's eyes meet mine, no doubt wondering if her apology eased my nerves.

Not that it would matter if it didn't. Like all good politicians, he's giving me the illusion of control.

At the end of the day, we both know I need him way more than he needs me. He can find another aspiring politician to marry his daughter tomorrow. But I can't find someone with the same connections he has.

Or someone people admire and hold in such high regard. The man is a legend in the industry because he's earned the respect of both parties, regardless of his own views.

He's also donated a shitload of money to my campaign, and without that, I'd have nothing.

Reminding myself of all I have riding on this and what I can't afford to lose, I nod.

"It's fine." I fix my mask and adjust my bowtie. "I'll get a few college brochures and approach Eden about it after the election is over. Maybe she'll be open to it after she does some research."

Milton and Margaret exchange smiles. Milton might be tough on his daughter, but everyone knows she's the one who has him wrapped around her finger.

"Sounds like a fine idea." Milton raises his glass. "You're gonna go far, Cain. Your father would be proud."

The room sways a little. "Thank you." I look at Margaret. "What do you say we put this argument behind us and dance?"

She takes the hand I'm holding out to her. "That would be lovely." She waves to Milton. "See you in a bit, Daddy."

He winks at me. "I'm going to talk to Judge Kennedy. Last I heard he's voting for your opponent, but we go way back so I have a feeling I can change his mind. He may even make a contribution to the cause."

"That would be amazing. Thank you, sir."

"Will that be before or after he locks you up?" a voice sneers behind me.

An ugly feeling crawls up my gut, and when I turn around, I know what—or rather *who*—is responsible for it. "Hello, Katrina."

Chapter 15
EDEN

My legs are shaking as I make my way up to the castle and I honestly feel like I'm going to pass out before I get to the entrance.

I can hear music coming from what must be the ballroom and I curse myself for all the mini-freak-outs I had while getting ready.

The last thing I want to do is draw attention to myself by walking in late.

Another wave of dizziness washes over me and just when I think I'm about to hit the pavement, I feel my phone vibrate.

Devil: There's a side-entrance you can go through. It's on the left side of the castle. It's unlocked.

I swear there are moments where Cain's so attuned to me it's almost like he knows me better than I know myself.

Speeding up my steps, I head toward the left side of the castle.

AngelBaby123: Almost there.
Devil: After you walk through the door, there's a short hallway. The ballroom will be on your right.

I reach the door after what feels like an eternity and continue down the hallway. The sound of music and people chattering makes my stomach churn.

In a few short steps, I'll be inside the ballroom with all of them.

AngelBaby123: I'm scared.

I curse under my breath. I'm supposed to be proving I can handle this.

Everything I want is right inside that room. Now isn't the time to be a baby.

Taking a deep breath, I force my legs to start walking.

My knees buckle as I enter. Even with the mask on I can't help but feel like everyone knows it's me.

I desperately search around for Cain, but it proves to be futile. It seems as if every man here is wearing the same black tux, bowtie, and inconspicuous black mask.

My phone vibrates.

Devil: You look beautiful.

I stop moving. *He can see me?*

I mentally smack myself on the head. Of course, Cain can see me. He purchased everything I'm wearing.

Including the string of pearls that glide across my most sensitive areas with the slightest of movements—making it downright impossible to forget what's under my dress.

AngelBaby123: Where are you?
Devil: Watching you.

I swear I blush five different shades of red. I know he didn't mean to sound dirty, but it sends a rush of heat between my legs anyway.

It also sends my anxiety into overdrive, because it reminds me I'm in a room full of people and not home in my bedroom.

Nerves flutter in my belly and I look down at the floor.

Every time I take in my surroundings, my head whirls like a cyclone. I feel much better staying on the sidelines, staring at my shoes.

Unfortunately, I end up crashing into a waiter holding a tray full of dishes.

My heart's in my throat when the tray wobbles. A second before it falls, a man comes out of nowhere and steadies it. Instead of a category five catastrophe, the only thing that hits the floor is a single glass.

The waiter looks relieved. I, however, am anything but. I've only been here a minute and already I'm causing problems. People are starting to stare.

"Thanks, man," the waiter says. "I owe you one."

"Don't mention it," a deep raspy voice replies.

"I'm so sorry." Nausea barrels into me as I bend down to pick up the broken glass. "I should have been paying better attention to where I was going—"

I freeze when a hand wraps around my wrist. "Let the waiter handle it."

I look up and all the oxygen gets sucked out of the room. I'm staring into the most intense blue eyes I've ever seen.

"You could hurt yourself if you're not careful."

I try to respond, but my throat goes dry. *Jesus.* It almost hurts to look at them head-on, like staring into an eclipse.

Transfixed, I take in the rest of his features. His complexion is tan, as if he spends most of his time in the sun. A jaw sharp enough to slice through metal is covered by a fine dusting of stubble. Not enough to be considered a beard, but a little more than a five o'clock shadow. His mouth has an interesting shape…almost pouty. Like he's sucking on a lemon. The rest of his face is shielded by a black mask, and I find myself grateful—because if the features I can see are *this* penetrating, I can't imagine what he looks like when all the puzzle pieces are put together.

My gaze drifts to his lips again, but the ink peeking out from under the collar of his tux catches my eye. His tattoos are out of place with the rest of his attire…make that the rest of the room.

Oddly enough, it's comforting. Like I'm not the only one who doesn't belong here.

Somehow, I manage to find my voice. "It's not a problem. It was my fault."

"What makes you so sure?"

I'm trying to think of how to answer that, but my finger starts throbbing. When I look down, I see blood.

"Guess you were right."

I look around for Cain because I know he's watching me, but the man turns my wrist, examining my finger. "There's a small piece of glass in there. Does it hurt?"

"Not really." I grimace. "A little."

I'm taken back when he brings my finger to his lips. I'm about to inform him that I don't need him to kiss my boo-boo, but to my utter bewilderment, he places my bloody finger in his mouth.

I'm too shocked to protest and too mesmerized to pull away. The breath I was holding leaves me in one big rush when he starts sucking. He's so gentle, so tender…it's almost erotic.

This is without a doubt the most unusual experience I've ever had in my life.

"It's out."

He stands, and I look down at my finger. It's barely even bleeding anymore.

"Thank you—" I start to say, but he's already gone.

Chapter 16
DAMIEN

"Thanks for saving my ass before. If there's anything I can do for you, or if there's something you need tonight, let me know."

Tearing my gaze away from the trembling fallen angel who's trying her best to blend in with the wall, I glare at the waiter. "How about you get the fuck out of my face and we'll call it even?"

His expression is comical, like he doesn't know whether to shit his pants or defend himself.

He's smarter than he looks though because he high tails it down the hallway.

I peer into the ballroom and focus my attention on my two favorite people.

Cain is still talking to his future father-in-law and new fiancée. Judging by the taut line of his jaw, the conversation isn't a pleasant one.

It's rather unfortunate…because his night is only going to get worse.

Swiveling my gaze to the other side of the room, I search for Eden.

She's not hard to spot…given she looks like a frightened kitten being held over water.

Christ, she's so uncomfortable, it's almost painful to witness.

Stroking my chin, I continue examining her. Even though her face is covered by a mask and she's unraveling at the seams…the girl is beautifully fascinating.

A breathtaking tragedy waiting to happen.

She reminds me of my fish when I put them in my tank for the first time.

Skittish in her new surroundings. Alone and exposed…despite being surrounded by her own kind.

Smirking, I reach down to adjust my growing erection.

And *vulnerable*…because she doesn't know there's a piranha watching her…and he's hungry.

My balls tingle when her lower lip trembles and her chest heaves, accentuating those full perky tits. Poor thing keeps checking her phone and looking around…desperate to connect with the man she's given her heart to.

The reason she's putting herself through all this torture.

My angel has no idea the man she loves is going to crush her soul before the night is over.

My dick twitches, straining against my zipper. It's like watching two trains about to collide…*boom.*

If I still had a heart, it would break for her. The girl didn't ask to be part of my plan…she's just an unfortunate casualty.

Cain, however—deserves everything coming to him.

Eden might be naïve…but Cain's the one at fault in this scenario due to his self-serving ways.

No matter who he has to step on or whose heart he has to break…Cain Carter always gets what he wants in the end.

Except this time.

Because I'm back…and I'm not leaving without getting what *I* want.

And what I want…is to teach him a lesson.

It's time Cain Carter learns what's it like to sacrifice.

What it's like to lose.

Grinding my molars, I crush the tiny sliver of glass in my mouth, wondering if Eden tastes as sweet as her blood does.

There's only one way to find out.

Pulling out my phone, I open the app and send a message.

Devil: How about I do something to help you relax?

Chapter 17
EDEN

Devil: How about I do something to help you relax?

I breathe a sigh of relief. I've been trying to get in contact with Cain since I've stepped inside the ballroom twenty minutes ago, but he hasn't responded until now.

I was beginning to think he was having second thoughts about us.

AngelBaby123: All I need is you. I'm near the DJ booth.
Devil: How about you meet me somewhere more private?
AngelBaby123: Okay. Where?
Devil: Go to the staircase in the atrium and take it to the second floor. When you reach the second floor, make a right and walk down the hallway. Third door on the left is a closet. I'll meet you in there.
AngelBaby123: You want me to meet you in a closet?
Devil: Yes.
Angelbaby123: Why?
Devil: I want to play with your pearls.

My pulse skitters. My entire body feels both lighter and heavier at the same time.

Devil: If you don't want to…
AngelBaby123: No, I do.
Devil: Then go upstairs. I'll give you further instructions after you get there.

My heart is beating out of my chest as I make my way up the large spiral staircase. The idea of meeting Cain in a closet during a party is equal parts exciting and nerve-wracking.

My legs are rubber by the time I find the door and turn the knob.

AngelBaby123: Here.

The closet is bigger than I thought it would be, but not big enough to be considered spacious. There's just enough room for two people to fit comfortably inside. I search for a light switch, but there isn't one.

A shudder runs through me at the same time my phone vibrates.

Devil: I want your ass facing the door.

My thighs clench as I turn around. I love this take-charge side of Cain.

AngelBaby123: Done.
Devil: Good. Now, listen to me carefully. What I say goes from this point on. Got it?
AngelBaby123: Okay.
Devil: I mean it, Eden. If you disobey me—I'll leave, and this will be over.
AngelBaby123: I understand.

Devil: Good girl.

Devil: After you put your phone on the floor, I want you to place both hands on the clothing bar above your head. Don't turn around and do not remove your hands from the bar unless you have my permission. I'll be there in sixty seconds.

I drop my phone and push the two jackets on the rack to the side.

Then I count to sixty.

The closet door opens at fifty-nine.

The woodsy scent of his aftershave is both familiar and reassuring and the tightness in my chest eases.

"Hi," I whisper into the darkness. The slight tremor in my voice echoes off the walls.

He doesn't respond.

I'm about to ask if something's wrong, but he presses himself against me.

My mouth goes dry when his cock nudges my ass. He's so hard for me. Just knowing he wants this as much as I do makes the tiny hairs on my arms stand on end.

"Cain?"

A bite to my shoulder blade makes me jolt. But just as quickly his tongue is soothing the sting.

I startle when he pushes the top of my dress down.

I don't know why I'm so jumpy. I've never been this nervous with Cain before. In fact, I'm usually the one who makes the first move.

Maybe that's what my problem is.

Since I can't remove my hands from where they are, I grind my ass against him. The movement causes delicious friction between my private parts and the pearls.

My grip on the bar tightens as the friction builds and he runs his calloused knuckles over my nipples, causing them to pucker. All my senses are heightened in here, making me even more sensitive than usual.

Chills erupt along my back when his big hand finds the slit in my dress and he walks his fingers up my thigh. Despite his unhurried actions, his touch feels a little rougher than last time, but not in a bad way.

Sweeping my hair to one side, he nuzzles my neck. His coarse stubble scrapes my skin as his hand climbs higher, drawing out my anticipation.

As much as I love what he's doing, it's becoming impossible not to touch him.

"Let me touch you." I draw in a jittery breath. "I want to make you feel good, too."

I'm prepared for him to refuse, but to my surprise, he takes one of my hands and brings it to his erection. Eagerly, I stroke him through his pants, loving the way his cock jerks under my palm.

Not able to wait another second, I tug his zipper down and slip my finger inside. He doesn't have underwear on. There's just warm, firm skin. Feeling bolder, I wrap my hand around his length and squeeze. He makes a low noise deep in his throat and the sound goes straight to my core. I go to pull him out fully, but he seizes my hand and places it on top of my other one.

I want to ask what he's doing, but it becomes clear when he binds both my wrists to the bar with some kind of silky cloth.

I swallow hard. "Is this a punishment or reward?"

His answer is a swift slap on my ass that makes me cry out.

"Both," he rasps, his gruff voice barely above a whisper. He must be as turned on as I am because it's even huskier than usual.

My pulse explodes when the hand inside my dress begins tracing the pearls of my G-string, applying gentle pressure along the way. It feels so good it drives me out of my mind.

"Cain—"

He plucks the string and hisses. The sensation is so sharp and unexpected my breath stalls.

Jesus. There's something incredibly sensual about being at someone else's mercy while they do whatever they want to you.

Dragging his teeth along my neck, he presses a pearl to my clit and rolls it. The ground beneath me tilts and I forget how to breathe.

He's so meticulous in his teasing, giving me tiny sparks of pleasure, but stopping before they blast off.

I'm so wound up I feel like I could burst any moment. "Please," I beg as he continues his delicious torture. "Put your finger inside me."

A growl escapes him, a dark one I've never heard before, but he doesn't grant me my request. Instead, he strokes the lips of my pussy with his knuckle, teasing.

Tension in my core tightens—every nerve ending in my body is begging for release.

"Please."

His teeth scrape my shoulder in warning, but I don't care. If he's not inside me soon, I'll go insane. It's agony not being able to see, touch, or hear him.

"I need to feel you."

The tip of his finger circles my opening, just barely enough to feel. My heart thuds against my ribs. It's a struggle to draw in air. I'm going to spontaneously combust if he makes me wait any longer.

"Cai—"

He plunges his finger inside me forcefully and I gasp, my heart pounding like a jackhammer.

I'm trying to catch my bearings when he slides it out…only to sink it back in a moment later, deeper this time.

I mewl and grind against him when he picks up speed and starts fucking me with his finger. Wet sounds fill the space between us, but I'm too focused on the amazing things he's doing to be embarrassed.

That is until he jams a second finger inside me, causing pressure my body wasn't prepared for, and I cry out in pain.

He freezes and my heart bottoms out. I don't want to ruin everything like I did last time.

"Don't stop," I choke out. "I can take it, I swear."

As if trying to prove my point, I clamp around him, trying to keep him inside me.

It doesn't work though because he removes them. The loss guts me. Me and my stupid virginity have blown it for the second time.

Pretty ironic for someone an entire town refers to as a whore.

A tear falls down my cheek and that only makes everything worse. I am completely mortified. I just want to get through this barrier between us, but it seems like it's never going to happen.

"I'm sor—"

The words stall in my throat when he gathers the hem of my dress and maneuvers it out of his way.

Then he drops to his knees.

My brows knit in confusion. I thought he was upset like last time. "What—"

He works his finger inside me again, much slower than before. A breath shudders out of me. This angle is deeper, and the new position steals my breath.

"Oh, God." I'm so wet I can feel it pooling between my thighs. He pushes me forward, causing the fabric to bite into my wrists, but I don't care, the pain only adds to my desire.

Red-hot pleasure slams into me when he parts my lips and spears me with his tongue.

"Cain—"

I yelp when he nips me before removing his mouth completely.

Tears prickle my eyes. I feel punished. Like he brought me to the highest of cliffs…only to push me off it.

"I'm sorry," I croak. My emotions have gone haywire and I don't know which end is up anymore. He's controlling every aspect of me. I'm starting to feel like a pet who is trying but failing miserably to please her owner. "I'm so sorry."

Nerves bunch in my stomach when he spreads me wider. I've never felt so vulnerable before.

"Shhh," he soothes, collecting my wetness on his thumb.

And just like that, my heart feels lighter. I'm basking in his warmth once more.

Until his thumb moves several inches and he presses a pearl to my puckered hole. I squirm, unsure what to make of the sensation. It feels amazing and scary at the same time.

My breathing hitches when he plants a kiss where the pearl is and his other hand comes around to cup my pussy.

Blood whooshes in my ears when he blows on the pearl and kisses me again.

And then he pauses.

I grow hot, my body sensing what he's about to do next. It's illicit and dirty and…

A guttural moan rips from my throat when his tongue replaces the pearl and his finger pumps inside my pussy. It's so unexpected, so enjoyable, my brain scrambles. Unlike his slow torture from before, this is carnal. He's eating me like the closet is the Sahara Desert and I'm the last drop of water that will ever touch his lips.

He groans, pushing his tongue in farther. *God.* He's like a ravenous, filthy caveman with no limits or restrictions. Every part of my body is his for the taking and I love it.

With a snarl, he pinches my clit between two fingers and swirls the tip of his tongue inside my ass, causing little floaty things to form in front of my eyes.

There's no way I'm going to last another minute with him doing this to me. My legs shake like trees in a hurricane. I can't hold on. This is too much. It feels too good.

"Cain." It's the first and only word to leave my lips before a tremble starts from my toes and transcends, picking up speed along the way, like a boulder rolling downhill.

I've had orgasms before, but this one rocks my entire body from the inside out. It's so extreme it's almost frightening. It pulls me in fifty different directions, chipping away at my foundation until I finally shatter.

It's so strong, it knocks the wind out of me. I don't have the strength to stand on my own, it literally wipes me off my feet.

I go slack against the restraints, but Cain wraps his arm around my waist and holds me steady, like he has for the last four years.

"I love you." I draw in a shaky breath. "I know that scares you and I know you don't feel things the same way I do—but I need you to know my feelings for you are real. It's not a crush, it's not misplaced affection, and it's not wrong."

He stands, but I continue. I need him to know how serious I am.

"Talking to you on the temptation app is the best part of my day," I whisper as he unties my wrists. "I've never been able to tell anyone the things I tell you and I never will." I grab the bar when my hands are free, remembering what he said about not moving until I had his permission. "I know you're worried about the election and you don't think I have what it takes to do this, but I do. I'll do anything in the world for you, Cain. I love—"

The sound of the door opening and closing cuts me off and I feel like a fool.

My heart twists when my phone vibrates a moment later. I pick it up with shaky fingers, petrified of what it will say.

Devil: Meet me on the dancefloor in five minutes.

And just like that, the organ in my chest takes flight. Cain was right…everything I wanted was here all along. All I had to do was reach out and take it.

Chapter 18
CAIN

Past...

"There's a fortune teller over there," Julia squeals as we enter the school gymnasium for the spring fling. "Can we?"

It's all I can do not to roll my eyes. "Sure."

She reaches for my hand. "We're gonna have so much fun tonight."

Considering it's our third date in two weeks and the only thing that's been in her mouth are those half chewed pens of hers…I doubt it.

Plastering a smile on my face, I take her hand and walk over.

My smile falls when the fortune teller takes off her masquerade mask.

"Hi, Mrs. Miller."

She doesn't miss a beat. "Hi, guys. Are you kids having fun?"

"We just got here," Julia answers, gesturing to the masquerade mask they handed her at the door. "I was hoping you could give me a reading."

"Sure. Both of you, or—"

"Just her," I say tersely. "I don't believe in this crap. There's no way a simple card can predict the future."

Julia frowns. "Yeah, you're right. This is stupid—"

"My grandmother used to say tarot cards don't predict your future, they simply hold up a mirror to your subconscious."

Julia's mouth drops open. "Your grandmother was a fortune teller too?"

I look up at the ceiling. "Mrs. Miller isn't a fortune teller, Julia. She's just a teacher chaperoning a dance."

She also happens to give one hell of a blow job.

Mrs. Miller points to her cards. "Actually, these were my grandmother's cards. She used to do this for a living."

"What a noble profession."

Mrs. Miller turns to Julia. "Don't let this negative nelly talk you out of it, it can be very enlightening."

Julia bites her lip, her stare ping-ponging between us. "I don't know."

"Do it." I shrug. "I think it's bullshit, but it's obvious you want to. Therefore, you should."

Her eyes gleam. "Okay. Do I have to do anything?"

Mrs. Miller hands her the deck of cards. "Shuffle these and concentrate on what you'd like the universe to tell you."

Out of the corner of my eye, I spot my brother talking with his friends. Or rather, they're all kissing his ass and congratulating him for the millionth time on getting a full ride to Harvard.

Jealousy snakes up my spine. I turned in my application two weeks before he did, and I still haven't heard back.

I wasn't worried until a few days ago when my friends on the debate team mentioned they all heard from their first and second choice schools.

Unlike them, I have no second choice. Harvard is it. It's where my father and all his friends went.

I'll never be able to live it down if my brother gets accepted, and I don't.

"Oh my God, that was so awesome," Julia screeches beside me, bringing me out of my thoughts. "I got the three of pentacles for my future and Mrs. Miller says that's a sign of great things ahead." She claps her hands. "She's right because I got my acceptance letter from Dartmouth today. It was my first choice."

My hands clench at my sides. *The girl who ingests the ink from her pens several times a week got accepted to her first college of choice and I didn't.*

I glance at my brother again and our eyes lock. I think he's about to call me over, but he nudges one of his friends who looks at me and winces.

Right before they start laughing their asses off. *Assholes.*

"I want a reading."

If Julia the pen whisperer's future is bright, then mine should be the motherfucking sun on steroids.

Mrs. Miller smiles. "Okay, sure."

Just like with Julia, she hands me the cards and tells me to concentrate while I shuffle them.

I give them back to her when I'm finished, and she turns over three of them. "These cards represent your past, present, and future." She gestures to the first card. "Your past is the king of swords. It represents a very forceful and opinionated man in your life. An authority figure who made you who you are today." Her brows knit together. "You learned to be responsible at a very early age and you take the lessons he instilled seriously."

Sounds about right. "Great. What's my future?"

As usual, it's my primary concern.

"Let me read your present first."

When she turns over the second card, Julia yelps, latching onto my arm for dear life. "No. Cain can't die."

Several heads turn to look at us.

I don't show it, but the ominous *death* card is a little unnerving to see.

"Relax. The death card doesn't mean Cain's going to die." She looks at me. "But it does mean you're going through a deep transformation and you're currently at a crossroads. But the thing about death is, just like the inevitable kind, it's impossible to fight.

The only thing you can do is let go and allow the changes to happen."

I raise a brow. "What changes?"

She points to the final card. "The future will give you more insight."

"Doubtful," I mutter. "Considering this reading hasn't been all that *insightful* to begin with."

"Oh," Julia says when Mrs. Miller turns over the final card. "It's…"

"The Devil," Mrs. Miller finishes for her.

Julia bends down for a closer look and blushes. "Um…are they—"

"Naked and bound?" Mrs. Miller nods. "Yup. The Devil is all about bondage." She clears her throat. "Metaphorically speaking of course." Her expression turns serious and she looks at me. "It's also a huge warning. When this card shows up in your future, it's cautioning you that something will go horribly wrong if you continue down the current path you're on." She starts ticking things off with her fingers. "Obsession, control, addiction, manipulation, temptation to evil…you're a slave to all of them."

"Nice cards," Damien interjects, walking out from behind the fortune teller booth. "Want to do me next?"

This time it's Mrs. Miller who blushes.

"Speak of the devil," I mutter, not surprised to see him at all.

"Hey, Julia. You're looking lovely as usual." He waggles his eyebrows. "Well, minus that ink spot on your dress." He leans in. "It's right—"

I smack the hand that's headed for her chest away. "Leave her alone, asshole."

Julia looks down at her shoes. "Can we go dance now, Cain?"

"Sure." I start to turn, but something hits my shoulder.

"Don't forget your mask," Damien taunts. "It is a masquerade party, after all."

Glaring at him, I bend down to pick up the mask. "Why are you here? I don't recall ever seeing you attend one of these."

Licking his lips, he puts on his own black mask. "What can I say? I'm all about new experiences." He jerks his chin toward the dance floor. "You guys have fun." Those creepy blue eyes land on me. "I'll just stand here and *watch*."

My ears get hot and I'm pretty sure they're about as red as the ink stain on Julia's dress.

I should have known Damien wasn't done with me yet.

Grabbing Julia's hand, I lead her out to the dance floor.

I feel Damien's eyes on me the entire time.

"Hi, Cain."

I inwardly groan at the sound of Katrina's voice. I can't even take a piss without her following me.

If I thought Damien was being a stalker, it has nothing on Katrina.

Monday, she called to say she was dropping off a box of my stuff.

Tuesday, she called to say she forgot to put a sweatshirt in the box and she'd meet me at my locker after school.

When I told her to keep it, she said she'd leave it on my porch instead.

Wednesday, she called to tell me her cat missed me.

And yesterday…she called to say she found a pencil of mine.

If she keeps it up—the next time she calls it will be to tell me she got served with a restraining order.

"Hi and goodbye." I go to walk past her, but she presses her hand to my chest.

"I'm sorry."

"You've said that about a hundred times since we broke up."

"Why are you being so mean to me?" Her eyes narrow. "Is it because you're dating Julia now?"

"I don't even know how to answer that."

"You don't have to. Just tell her it's over and we can pick up where we left off."

"With you screwing someone else behind my back? Nah, I'm good."

I try to leave again, but she stands in front of me. "I never should have cheated on you."

"And I never should have eaten four-day-old pizza last week. Shit happens, move on." I start walking toward the gymnasium where Julia's waiting for me. "I have."

Julia is the one thing in my life as of late that my father approves of and I'm not letting go of her. Not until I get my acceptance letter from Harvard and tell my brother and everyone else who doesn't believe in me to suck it.

"Ouch," Damien says when I pass him. "That was harsh." His voice lowers. "What do you say we take her out to the shed, bend her over, and teach her a lesson?"

I ignore the tightening in my groin. "Fuck off."

"I'm gonna go to the little girls' room. Can you grab me some punch?"

I'm already halfway to the table. "Got it."

I'm starting to wish I had a few pens to shove in her mouth so she'd shut the fuck up. How one single person can be so infuriatingly annoying is beyond me.

"Trouble in paradise?"

It's so bad I don't mind talking to Damien. Then again, it's not like I have much of a choice. He's one of the only few people still here.

I set two cups on the table. "She wants to stay until the end to help clean up…and then go for ice cream after."

"Is ice cream code for blow job?"

"I wish." I wince. "On second thought, I take that back."

Damien smirks. "Not that brave, huh?"

I pick up the ladle. "Not that desperate."

"Let me help you out." He opens his jacket and takes out a bottle. "It's only vodka, but it will take the edge off."

Before I can object, he pours some in the cups.

"I'm driving."

He shrugs, typing a message on his phone. "So give them both to her."

Not a bad idea. Maybe now she'll be quiet.

Leaning against the table, I study him. "Not to be a dick, but why are you here? You didn't bring a date. And the only people I've seen you talk to tonight are me and Mrs. Miller."

He takes a sip of the drink in his hand. "Been watching me, have you?"

"No." I bring one of the cups to my lips. "And even if that was the case, you're one to talk."

His lips twitch. "Well, unlike you I'm not a hypocrite who runs from something that intrigues him." He tucks his phone in his back pocket. "And according to the very extensive reading I got from Kristy tonight, I can be very persistent when I want something."

I roll my eyes. "Please don't tell me you believe in that crap."

"I don't know." He looks across the room. "She's into it."

I follow his gaze to the fortune booth where Mrs. Miller's packing up shop. "So, what…is she your girlfriend or something?"

The corners of his eyes crinkle. "Or something." He places his cup on the table. "I don't do girlfriends. But she is my favorite."

"I can tell."

When he raises an eyebrow I mumble, "The texts."

"What can I say?" His lips curve into a smirk. "I like things I shouldn't. The more taboo, the better."

"Do you ever get nervous?" I take another swig of my drink. "You know, about her husband finding out."

"No. That's her shit, not mine."

Fair enough. Out of the corner of my eye, I spot Julia enter the gymnasium. "My date's back."

He salutes me. "Only thirty minutes left."

"Thank God."

I start to leave, but he taps my shoulder. "You never asked me what my plans are after the dance."

I blink. "What are your plans after the dance?"

He crooks a finger. When I lean in, he whispers, "I'm going to tie Mrs. Miller to my bedpost and cram my dick down her throat." His lips ghost over my ear. "And then I'm going to fuck her so hard she squirts all over my two-thousand-dollar sheets."

My balls tingle and I hate him for telling me this. "Good for you, man."

"You're welcome to join us. We can double team her. I take the back, you take the front." He jerks his chin toward Julia. "Or you can eat ice cream and pens with pica girl." His gaze drifts to Mrs. Miller who's almost done packing. "I'm leaving in ten."

My palms grow damp. The fact that I'm already thinking of ways to ditch Julia speaks volumes. But I can't. It's bad enough I jerk off several times a day while reliving what happened in that classroom. If I fall down this rabbit hole, there's no coming back. I can kiss my future goodbye.

"Pass. Thanks for the offer though."

"That's too bad." He looks at Mrs. Miller and grins. "Fortune favors the bold."

"Do you think Kim's new haircut is weird?" Julia questions as we sway to the music. We're one out of three couples left on the dance floor.

"Do you think it's weird?"

I've learned the best way to answer her questions is to direct them back to her.

"A little. Her bangs are kind of short." She purses her lips. "Then again they'll grow out, so I guess it really doesn't matter."

"Nope." *Nothing about this conversation matters.*

In my peripheral vision, I spot Mrs. Miller leaving the gymnasium. Damien hangs back by the bleachers, looking between me and his watch every so often.

"What did you think about the dress Stacy Saxton wore on Tuesday?"

I grit my teeth. "What did *you* think about the dress?"

I scan the bleachers. My blood quickens when I realize he's no longer there but moving toward the exit.

Julia scrunches her face, pondering. "I'm not sure."

Damien casts me one last glance…

And then he's gone.

"I think it made her look a little chubby, but it was an unflattering c—"

"Fuck," I yell before I double over.

"Oh my God. Cain, what's wrong?"

"I think I'm dying." It's not a lie. I'm positive I'm going to keel over if she asks me one more goddamn question about Stacy or Kim and their stupid wardrobe.

"What?" Julia shrieks. "Holy crap, the card was right."

Clutching my stomach, I hobble toward the exit. "I think I have food poisoning." I dig my keys out of my pocket and hand them to her. "I don't want you to catch this. You should take my car and drive yourself home."

She stares at me like I've sprouted another head. "You want me to drive your car?"

"Yup." *Drive it off a goddamn bridge for all I care.* "I'm not sure how long I'll be in the bathroom. I'll get a ride home from my brother later."

I break into a sprint. Hopefully Damien didn't leave yet.

"Wait," she screeches. "Does this mean we're going steady? Am I your girlfriend?"

"Sure. Whatever."

The second I'm outside the gymnasium I start running like a football player heading for the end zone.

"Wait up."

"Well, I'll be damned." Damien's eyes widen when he sees me. "Look who decided to stop being a pussy."

"This better be worth it. I'm pretty sure I just gave Julia my car so she'd leave me alone."

"Fuck that bitch." He bangs the side of his truck. "Get in, fucker. Good pussy waits for no one." Jumping into the driver's seat, he revs the engine. "Kristy only has two hours before her husband gets home from his fishing trip."

I open the passenger side door and climb inside. "I'm pretty sure we're going to hell."

"I own a timeshare there." He flashes me a quick evil grin as he shifts the car into drive. "The weather's beautiful this time of year."

Chapter 19

CAIN

"Don't you Hello Katrina me, asshole. I spoke to the Independent Chronicle earlier and they said the last time they spoke to Jodie was before she left the office to go to your house."

Milton frowns. "Is this true?"

I swallow hard. "Yes, she was conducting an interview with Eden."

"Right," Katrina says, and I notice she's slurring her words. The drink in her hand is half empty, but I'm willing to bet my next paycheck it's not her first of the night. Not her second or third either. "She had an interview at your house and then she vanished after." Her drink splashes over the rim. "Well, not before *you* went on a rampage, kicked her out, and got her fired."

"Her questions were inappropriate and upsetting my step-daughter."

"Oh, please. That's rich coming from *you* of all people."

I can feel everyone's eyes on us now. "Look, Katrina, I know you and your husband—" I look at the man beside her. If memory serves, he's an assistant to the DA. *Fuck.* "Are concerned about—"

"So concerned they're attending a party while their daughter is missing," Margaret interjects.

Katrina's mouth drops open. "How *dare* you."

"How dare I what? Tell you what everyone here is thinking? I might not have children, but I do know if I were missing, the last place my father—the *governor*—would be is at a party."

Milton nods. "My daughter is absolutely correct. I'm sorry for what you're going through, but it doesn't give you the right to point fingers and attack an innocent man. I've known Cain since he was born and he would never hurt anyone. I suggest you go home, sober up, and focus on finding your daughter."

The crushing feeling in my chest dissipates a little. When Governor Bexley speaks, people listen.

Katrina's husband takes hold of her elbow. "Come on, Katrina. I think we're done here. Let's go home."

Evidently, Katrina doesn't agree because she gets close to my face. "Your sweet mayor act won't work on me."

Straightening my spine, I look her right in the eyes. "Katrina you're emotional and—"

"Still carrying a torch for you," Margaret cuts in with a flick of her wrist. "Everyone in town knows you cheated on Cain and followed him around like a desperate puppy for years when he wouldn't take you back." She grabs my hand. "Sorry, Katrina, but he's taken. Now I suggest you take your husband's advice and go home before you embarrass yourself even more."

Maybe marrying Margaret isn't such a bad idea after all. She can certainly hold her own.

"Let's go," her husband barks.

Katrina shakes her head. "So help me God if you had anything to do with my stepdaughter's disappearance, I will end you."

Keeping my expression impassive, I look at the security guard standing in the corner of the room.

Margaret's grip on my hand tightens. "You don't have to stand here and take this. Let's go dance."

"Just you wait," Katrina shouts as the security guard escorts her out. "After he's done using you, he'll dump your ass."

Chapter 20
CAIN

Past...

Mrs. Miller twists against her restraints. "I'm not sure." Her chest heaves, lifting those heavy tits high. "I can't see either of you with this blindfold on."

Damien circles her nipple with the tip of his finger. "You can't?" He looks at me and I give it a little flick with my tongue. "Such a shame."

Damien tsks. "I thought you were a fortune teller, Mrs. Miller?" He slaps her tit and it jiggles against my mouth. "What do you say we try this one more time?" Pushing his hips forward, he sinks inside her. "Whose cock is this?"

You'd think it would be weird sharing with another guy, but it's not. If anything, it adds to the thrill of the illicit act. I'm starting to see why Damien prefers screwing women he shouldn't.

"Come on, Kristy. Is it me or Cain?"

"I don't know."

He slams into her and she moans. "Oh, fuck."

I pinch her nipple. "It's like you're not even trying, Mrs. Miller."

She starts to answer, but Damien withdraws himself and we

switch places. We've been playing this little game with her for the last hour. Every time she attempts to answer, we change positions.

And then we tease her all over again.

Slowly, I proceed to feed her my cock. "Good girls get rewarded."

Lowering his head, Damien blows on her pussy. "You want to be rewarded, don't you?"

The cool air sends a tingle through my balls and I shift uncomfortably. I know he's only toying with her, but his mouth is dangerously close to my junk. And while Damien and I might have similar sexual interests, and I don't mind sharing her with him—I'm not into dudes. I'm pretty sure he's not either, considering he fucks everything in a skirt.

"Yes," Mrs. Miller rasps. "I want you both to make me come."

He purses his lips. "Then tell us who's inside you."

Chills race over my skin when he does it again. It's hard not to have a physical reaction when your cock is buried to the hilt inside a cunt and someone else's mouth is hovering over it…blasting air.

Eyes on me, his mouth inches closer to her pussy. "Answer the question, Mrs. Miller."

Nerves zip up my spine. My breathing turns choppy. One wrong move and he'll be touching us both.

He nips her pubic bone and she hisses. "I don't know. You both have big dicks."

That has us grinning.

Parting her lips with two of his fingers, he strikes her clit with the tip of his tongue. "We appreciate the compliment, but we're still not letting you come until you tell us whose big dick is inside you."

But she won't, because that's part of the game.

When she doesn't answer, he repeats the movement, only this time he sucks the entire bud into his mouth, causing his lips to ghost over my shaft.

I freeze. However, my dick twitches, clearly not opposed to the action.

"Please." Her hips buck and I groan. "I want to come so bad."

He releases her clit with a wet plop. "That's up to Cain."

I swallow hard.

Smirking, Damien plants a kiss above her pussy. "Look at this hot little cunt, just begging to be eaten properly." His kisses descend. "Don't you think she deserves that, Cain?"

"Pretty please," Mrs. Miller begs as Damien's tongue circles her clit.

I pull back slightly, giving Damien more room to work.

"Oh, fuck."

Whatever he's doing to her must feel great because she mewls and clamps my tip like a vise.

Damien's mouth edges closer, the corners of his lips tickling my skin. A low grunt rips from my throat and we stare at one another, both of us panting. His gaze drops to my glistening dick, half of which is still buried inside our teacher.

His eyes darken.

I can't tell if it's a challenge, or if he's offering me an out.

I draw in a lungful of air. *Why am I so freaked out about this?*

It's not like it's the other way around. A mouth is a mouth. And this mouth isn't mine, so it doesn't matter where it goes. If Damien wants to up the ante for himself, I'm not going to stand in his way. Besides, everyone in the room knows I'm only here for the pussy.

He tears his gaze away and I watch as he continues working over Mrs. Miller's swollen bud. Blood rushes in my ears, the anticipation of what he's about to do—or not going to do—has my dick throbbing so hard I feel like I could nut from that alone.

Which is strange as hell, because I enjoy having all the control. Yet here I am, wondering if Damien's mouth is ever going to move that half a centimeter.

Shame slams into me, because it's not something I should be thinking…but it's washed away by white-hot pleasure when his tongue slides along my length for the briefest of moments before going back to licking her pussy.

Heat sears my skin and I stop breathing.

Damien's lips curve into a smirk. "You like that?"

My retort stalls in my throat—and thank fuck—because I realize he's talking to Mrs. Miller.

"Yes, I'm so close. Don't stop."

My throat bobs on a swallow and right when I'm about to start thrusting because I have to release all this pent-up tension, his tongue glides up and down my shaft again…slower this time.

My whole body vibrates in response.

"Fuck," I groan. I'm suddenly thankful he had the good sense to blindfold Mrs. Miller because I grab the bedsheets, coming so hard the bed shakes.

And Damien—the fucker—continues licking her pussy filled with my cream, causing aftershocks that have my head spinning.

A few moments later, Mrs. Miller orgasms and Damien shoots his load all over her face before he unties her.

I, however, am lying on the bed, wondering what the hell just happened and how I got here. If someone told me three weeks ago that Damien King would play a part in the best sexual experience I've ever had, I'd kick them in the junk and tell them to get a psych evaluation.

"Crap," Mrs. Miller says after she wipes off her face. "I'm late. Chad's home already."

Damien reaches across his nightstand for his cigarettes. "Tell him you stayed after the dance to clean up."

"Good idea." She gathers her things and blows us both a kiss. "Take care, boys. Be good."

"And that," Damien says after the door closes behind her. "Is why she's my favorite." He takes a long drag off his cigarette. "She doesn't overstay her welcome."

I start to get off the bed, but he shakes his head. "Relax, that wasn't a dig. Bros over hoes, remember?"

Taking the cigarette from his hand, I bring it to my lips and inhale. Surprisingly, Damien doesn't laugh or make fun of me when I start coughing. He just takes another one out of the pack and lights it.

And that's how we stay for a while. Sitting in the dark, chain-smoking—while staring at his gigantic neon-lit fish tank.

"What kind of fish is that?"

The tank alone has to be at least two-hundred gallons, it's strange he would opt to only have a single fish in it. Although the fish is kind of cool looking.

"Red-bellied piranha."

I look for signs he's joking, but there are none. "I don't know if that makes you a bad-ass or a psychopath. Don't they eat humans?"

He blows out a thick line of smoke. "Nah. Most species of piranhas are harmless. There are only two types that attack humans."

"What are they?"

"Black piranhas." A menacing smirk unfurls, and his eyes harden. "And red-bellied piranhas."

I recoil, wondering if I should attack first and ask questions later.

His lips quirk. "Don't worry, he was fed recently." When I make a face, he laughs and says, "Fish. Not humans."

"What made you choose a piranha in the first place?"

His expression goes slack and I swear the room drops a few degrees. "My mom. I lived with her before she kicked the bucket and I moved in with my dad." His jaw sets. "Long story short, she was a dope head. Wasn't much of a mother. Most of the time she forgot I existed."

He reaches for a bottle of Jack Daniels on the nightstand and takes a swig. "I went hungry more often than not. But my mom…" He laughs, but there's not a drop of humor. "She was obsessed with these fucking fish. The only time she'd pay me any attention was to remind me to feed them before she shot up."

He drags a hand over his scalp. "It was always, 'feed my fish for me, Damien,' and 'Damien, don't forget to feed my fish.' The bitch was obsessed." He shrugs. "But I did it. No matter how many days she was gone. No matter how hungry or lonely I became…I always made sure to feed her goddamn fish. Because it was her thing…the only thing she ever gave a shit about other than dope." His expression turns solemn. "On my thirteenth birthday, my father sent me fifty bucks like he did every year. And as usual, she got to it before I could. She spent forty-five dollars on dope and five on fish food. Left none for her son."

His eyes become glassy and he clears his throat. "The dope she bought with it must have been powerful because when I came home from school, I found her dead on the kitchen floor." He draws in a deep breath and lets it out slowly. "After I called an ambulance, I walked down to the local aquarium store for some more fish food, but something else caught my eye. The owner of the store was pretty cool, usually gave me a lot of stuff for free, and when I told him I wanted it, he said it was mine."

The hairs on my neck lift as he continues. "I ran back home before the ambulance got there and kissed my mother goodbye. Then, I walked over to the pretty fish and gave them some food." His eyes crinkle at the corners. "While they were eating, I dumped my new red-bellied piranha in the tank." His teeth flash white. "And fed my fish."

Chapter 21
CAIN

"That woman is a headcase," Margaret says as we make our way to the dance floor. "Thank God security tossed her out."

"Her hysterics certainly didn't earn me any new voters, that's for sure." I place my hands on her waist as the next song queues up. I never noticed until now, but Margaret's not bad to look at. Her raven hair and porcelain skin is an arresting combination in the right light. "I appreciate you coming to my rescue."

We begin dancing, but thanks to my two left feet, I bump into someone. I'm not sure who though because all I see is a flash of black and red as they scurry off the dance floor.

"Daddy thinks very highly of you." Margaret's expression turns serious. "He's ecstatic you're going to be his son-in-law."

"The feeling is mutual." I spin us around and a woman standing nearby catches my eye. She's wearing a striking black and red dress. "Your father is a good man."

Margaret clasps her hands around my neck, pulling me closer. "What about you?"

"Pardon?" I'm trying to pay attention, but the other woman snags every ounce of my focus.

"Katrina's a bitch, but she was right about one thing. Your track record when it comes to love isn't the greatest. Arrangement or not, I don't want to marry you for all the wrong reasons. I'm the kind of girl who needs some of the right ones."

"Right."

"I won't be made to look like a fool like all your other exes."

I can't see her face because she's wearing a mask like the rest of us. Not that it matters…she's utterly captivating.

She's got the kind of body men worship—and the dress she's wearing hugs her curves in all the right places.

My heart races as I continue my assessment. Her red lips are plump and heart-shaped, and her long legs seem to go on for miles thanks to the sexy dress, sheer black stockings, and high heels. Her long blonde hair falls down her back in loose tendrils. She has the kind of hair a man wants to run his hands through while kissing her.

The kind of hair you want to wrap around her throat and pull while you fuck her.

Given all the heads that are turning in her direction, other people are starting to notice her too. Probably wondering who she is like I am.

Margaret, appearing frustrated with my inability to hold a conversation, stops dancing. "I know you're close with my father—but are you a good guy like he is? Or are you planning on using him and hurting me after you get what you want?"

Fuck. The last thing I need after Katrina's episode is for Margaret to have second thoughts. Anyone standing near us earlier already heard her declare we're an item.

If the governor's daughter ends things with me right before the election, it will make voters wonder why. *It will make them doubt me.*

"No." My throat feels like sawdust. "I'm a good guy." I give her a boyish grin. "Just a little unlucky when it comes to love." I skim a finger up her arm. "I'm hoping the right woman can change that."

She blushes. "Well, if that's the case, why don't we find out?"

I'm about to ask what she means, but she closes the distance between us and kisses me. A public kiss wasn't part of the plan for tonight, but I'm not about to dismiss her advances when we'll be announcing our engagement shortly.

Therefore, I do what I've always done. Put on my other mask… and play the role I'm supposed to.

Cupping her cheek, I kiss her like I mean it. Like she's my everything. Evidently, I'm a little too convincing because there are some claps and cheers.

Margaret, playing her own role, feigns the perfect mixture of embarrassment and happiness as she rests her head on my shoulder.

"What do you say we go somewhere more private?" I'm about to decline because we're at a public event, but she whispers, "I want to take care of my future husband the way a wife should…with my mouth."

I look around before I give her my answer, "Meet me upstairs in five minutes."

With that, I turn around and start walking…

And end up bumping into the woman in the black and red dress for the second time that night. She looks different from before. Sadder.

"Sorry," I toss out behind me, heading for the stairs.

It's only after I'm entering an empty bedroom that I realize her eyes were glassy. As though she'd been crying.

Chapter 22
CAIN

Past...

"I'm so close." Her breasts bounce. Her back arches. Her cunt clenches. "Please."

"You'll come when we're ready," Damien tells her, licking a line along her slit. Her hands and legs are bound, giving us easy access to do whatever we please.

When he pulls back, I lean in. "So impatient."

Mrs. Miller moans. "Please, I'll do anything you want."

I slide my tongue inside her heat. "What do you mean *anything*?"

"Any naughty thing you want." Despite being blindfolded, she looks down. "Name it."

I pull my mouth away as Damien comes forward again, planting a kiss on her clit. "Will you give me and Cain rim jobs?"

I blink. That's...*intense*. And definitely not something I've experienced before. Although I've watched Damien do it to Mrs. Miller a few times. Usually while I'm pounding her out.

Mrs. Miller's down for almost anything, but I'm not sure she'd go for something like that.

"I'll do it to whoever makes me come first."

Well, shit. I stand corrected.

Without thinking, I tilt my head and flick her pussy at the same time Damien does. Our tongues nearly touch.

He pauses and embarrassment courses through me. My only choice is to goad him and play it off as a dare. "What's the matter? Afraid of a little competition?"

He laughs darkly. "We both know I'm not a chicken shit." He circles her asshole with his thumb and looks down at my hardening dick. "Unlike you, I have no sexual limits."

With that, he goes back to eating her out.

My blood burns. Damien's managed to stir the beast. If there's one thing I hate more than being teased and ridiculed…it's losing.

Edging forward, I crowd his space, spearing my portion of her cunt with my tongue. Not one to back down either, Damien laps her clit frantically.

I match his speed, but he's got the leverage since he's currently working the spot that guarantees he'll win.

As if proving my point, Mrs. Miller goes fucking crazy. Screaming so loud I'm regretting not gagging her.

Rage simmers beneath the surface, lighting me up. But that changes to arousal when Damien's tongue brushes mine.

I tense, and Damien makes a low hum in the back of his throat, mocking me.

Not one to concede, I up the ante. The next time his tongue peeks out I nudge it with mine.

He freezes.

Smirking, I take the opportunity to pick up the slack, attacking Mrs. Miller's clit like I'm a man on death row and this is the last pussy I'll ever taste.

She whimpers and bucks her hips. "Oh God. That's it. I'm so close. Please don't stop."

Feeling satisfied I'm going to win, I accelerate, flicking my tongue so fast I feel like the damn thing is going to fall off.

That is until Damien's tongue glides across mine, licking us both. And this time, it's not a quick strike—he slides it inside my mouth, intentionally taunting me.

The leverage I gained starts slipping and to my absolute horror, my dick twitches.

Unwilling to accept defeat, I rise to the challenge, massaging his tongue with mine.

He grunts. Mrs. Miller goes nuts.

And I'm happier than a pig in shit, because I know I'm going to win this round.

Until Damien's hand moves up my thigh, creeping toward my dick.

I still. My balls jolt.

Damien, the fucker, carries on; licking us both while his thumb teases the now throbbing head peeking out of my boxers.

"That feels so good," Mrs. Miller yells as he continues pleasuring her. "Right there."

Heat zips up my spine when he pulls on the waistband of my boxers and my erection springs out, slapping my stomach.

Part of me hates what he's doing, but the other half doesn't want him to stop what he started.

Mrs. Miller sounds like she's getting closer and closer. I drive my tongue between his open mouth and her clit, desperate not to lose.

His hand wraps around my dick and I stop breathing. I don't care who gets me off at this point, all I know is it better happen soon.

He strokes me from root to tip. "Is this what you want?"

"Yes," Mrs. Miller screams, unable to see the other situation developing below her due to the blindfold. "I'm gonna come soon."

I thrust into his hand, unable to stop the train that's officially left the station. Even if I lose the battle of making Mrs. Miller come, I'll win the war if I come and Damien doesn't.

He picks up his pace, stroking me so fast it nearly burns. I groan into his mouth, digging my nails into the carpet we're both kneeling on while Damien keeps working the both of us.

"I'm coming," Mrs. Miller announces a minute before she starts convulsing. A strangled sound leaves me when Damien grabs the back of my neck and shoves his tongue into my mouth, right before he pushes me to the floor and gets on top of me.

Jesus Christ. He's full on kissing me now. I don't know whether I want to puke or come.

I can't even move if I wanted to because he pins my arms above my head, grinding his dick against my hard-on. I hate his stupid father for building that fucking gym.

I groan when his mouth descends down my torso. I swear to God if he's intentionally taunting me when I'm at my weakest, I will shove a goddamn stake right through his heart, push my dick in his mouth, and watch him bleed out like the motherfucking devil he is.

He nips my abs, intentionally avoiding my cock. Rage races through me again and I grind my teeth.

My hands which are free now go to his head, but he's quicker than I am because he maneuvers out of the way at the last moment.

He straddles me, and I notice Mrs. Miller's panties are in his hand. I'm about to ask what he's doing, but faster than I can blink, he secures my wrists with them.

I buck my hips, trying to get out from underneath him, but he shifts his weight on top of me, his lips hovering over my ear. "If you want it in my mouth, you better beg me like a good boy."

"I'm not begging you for shit." His hand wraps around me again and he swirls the pre-cum around my tip with his thumb. "Fuck."

I flinch when I realize Mrs. Miller's still tied to the bed. She can't see what's going on, but she's probably starting to wonder what we're doing. Damien's out of his teacher fucking mind if he thinks I'm going to beg him for a blow job in general, let alone in front of a woman. Especially when I'm being restrained by a pair of panties.

Grunting, I drive into his hand. If he's going to keep jerking me, I might as well get some fucking enjoyment out of it. Hell, maybe karma will take pity on me and I'll end up spraying my load all over him.

Teach the faggot a lesson he'll never forget.

He bites a line from my neck to my jaw, sending little zings of pleasure straight to my cock. My chest rises and falls, struggling to get enough air into my lungs as he works his hand up and down my shaft. I'm seething, the wrath I carry around daily surging into something dark and ugly. I dig my teeth into his bottom lip until I taste blood, but that only makes him grin. "Now we're talking."

I open my mouth to tell him to fuck off, but he sweeps his tongue inside, like the serpent he is. When I resist, the hand on my dick grips my balls, forcing me to open my mouth wider. Our teeth clash, and I shove my tongue down his throat, hoping he'll choke on it.

However, it only entices him, and he starts sucking mine, provoking me.

"Suck my cock just like that," I growl into his mouth. "You fucking pussy."

I should have learned my lesson about daring Damien from earlier because his finger brushes the hot spot between my balls and ass and I shudder.

"Let me hear you beg."

Swear on everything, I hate Damien King with the fire of ten thousand suns.

Swallowing my pride, I murmur, "Please, suck the cum out of my dick." I drag my teeth along the shell of his ear. "If you don't... I'll walk over to your precious Mrs. Miller and stuff it down her throat until she suffocates."

Panic lashes through me the second the words leave my mouth —I've never let anyone see the volcano of evil I keep deep down inside—but it quickly turns to pain when he elbows me in the stomach...and then satisfaction when his hand grips my throat and he lowers his mouth to my cock.

My heart beats out of my chest as he sucks me hard and fast, the pain giving way to pleasure.

My balls lift and my hips spasm as he draws every ounce of cum from my cock and swallows it.

I watch him with cautious eyes as he rises above me, his hand pumping his own dick wildly.

My stomach drops when a slow, malicious grin spreads across his face, and I feel something wet hit my thighs.

Horrified, I look down as another rope of cum lands on my now flaccid dick. His wicked grin grows as he rubs it into my pubic hair, leaving his mark.

~

"Bye, boys. Be good," Mrs. Miller says before she blows us a kiss and closes the door behind her.

An awkward silence fills the room in her absence. Grabbing my clothes, I start getting dressed.

"Wonder if she realizes her panties are missing," Damien drawls, lighting a cigarette.

I laugh, grateful for the diversion. "Hopefully her husband doesn't realize."

He lights another cigarette and hands it to me. "I'll shoot her a text in a few."

I can feel his eyes on me as I take a long drag. "Look, I didn't mean what I said before, okay?"

There. I acknowledged the first elephant in the room. Maybe we can put this past us.

He doesn't say a word.

Mortified, I reach for my keys and wallet. "Fuck you, Damien."

I'm halfway to the door when he finally speaks. "Why? Because you liked it?"

My hands clench into fists at my sides. "If that shit ever happens again this fucked up friendship of ours is over."

~

It's been three days since the incident. Damien goes about his business, acting like it never happened.

But me? It's all I can think about.

Why did I let him do it? Why didn't I stop him?

Does Mrs. Miller know what happened? Sure, she was tied up and blindfolded, but she's not deaf.

If something like this ever got out, it would ruin me for good. My father and brother would disown me…my dreams would be tarnished, and my life as I knew it would be over.

And yet, I can't seem to make myself stop hanging around Damien.

He gets me in a way other people don't. Almost like he has the same sickness I do buried inside him. Only, he shows everyone who he is. He's not ashamed of the things he likes…the things he does.

He's free. Because he doesn't give a shit about anything.

Then again, it's easy not to care when you have nothing to lose.

Damien's going nowhere in life. But me? I've got plans.

"Fuck me harder," Mrs. Miller screams.

"Shut the fuck up, Kristy." I yank her hair so hard I'm surprised it doesn't tear right off her scalp. I'm getting tired of her demands. Tired of not hearing from Harvard. Tired of my father's punches and my brother's snickering.

So fucking tired.

Every day that goes by, I'm closer to snapping.

Mrs. Miller flinches and a sharp bite to my thigh makes me hiss.

Most of Damien's face is covered because Mrs. Miller's riding it while I fuck her asshole, but his eyes are visible.

And right now, they're flashing me a warning. *Be easy*.

He's such a goddamn hypocrite. He's pulled her hair and told her to shut up plenty of times. Only when *he* does it, she doesn't flinch like a little prissy baby who can't take a dick.

There's a certain level of trust between them that doesn't exist between us. Which is fine by me, it's not like I give a fuck about her.

It just pisses me off when he comes to her defense and has the nerve to give me shit for doing the same stuff he does.

I'm getting tired of being the third wheel in this little shitshow.

So fucking tired.

And if she's going to cry like a little bitch, maybe I should give her something to cry about.

I yank her hair again, but she yells, "My phone is ringing." She freezes. "That's my husband's ringtone."

"Not my problem." If she's quiet, I'll be through with her in five minutes. "I'm not done with you yet."

"He's supposed to be at practice. Something must have come up. I have to find out what's going on."

"Not." *Thrust.* "My." *Thrust.* "Problem."

"Cain this is serious. I have to answer that."

Ignoring her, I thrust harder.

"Please."

"Say please one more fucking—"

A sharp punch to my thigh has me stumbling back. "What the fuck?"

Damien lurches up from the bed. "Let her answer her phone."

"I wasn't done yet."

"None of us were."

Venom rushes through my veins. A vision of me standing on the sidelines while he's screwing my girlfriend until *he* comes flashes through my head. As usual, Damien's a fucking hypocrite.

"She's the whore who cheats on her husband, not me." I point to my chest. "Why should I be punished?" I narrow my eyes. "And you're one to fucking talk—"

The sound of a door slamming cuts me off mid-sentence.

"Did that cunt really just leave?" I charge for the door, but Damien pulls me back.

"Chill."

"No." When I try to punch him, he wrestles me to the floor. "I'm gonna drag her back here by her hair and make her finish me off."

Seething, I bolt up, but he slams me back down and sits on my legs. "She's already gone."

The sound of a car starting in the distance makes me grit my teeth. I hate when he's right, but I hate being revved up with nowhere to go even more. I need an outlet. I need somewhere to channel all this indignation bubbling inside my chest.

I look down. Damien's hand is hovering above my throat, ready to strike at any moment. *Like he knows I'm a second away from losing my shit entirely.*

I hate the way Damien tries to control me. *He's starting to remind me of my father.*

My ears ring with fury and I lunge for him. I want to scratch his creepy eyeballs out and feed them to his goddamn piranha. *Hell, I just might.*

As usual, I underestimated Damien's strength, because he shifts his weight and pins my arms to the floor.

"Calm the fuck down."

"Make me."

My stomach sours when his eyes flash with heat, mistaking my exasperation as an invitation, but my cock thickens when his hips rub against mine.

Releasing one of my arms, he reaches between us, grazing my erection. "That for me?"

"Didn't think you were the type to ask for permission. What's next? You gonna paint my nails?"

Grunting, he licks a line from my Adam's apple to my jaw. "I'll ask you one more time, asshole." The hand on my dick squeezes. "Is this for *me*?"

There's only one way out of this. One solution at my disposal. One way to put an end to the torment.

"Only if you can make it come."

He smirks. "We both know I can make it and *you* do whatever I want." He licks the seam of my lips. "Open."

When I refuse, he laughs.

The joke's on me when I realize he's securing my wrist.

I struggle against his hold. "No—" The moment my mouth opens his tongue strikes. Our mouths battle, dueling it out for control as he ties both my wrists together.

"Good boy."

My breathing accelerates as he lowers his head, sucking and biting his way down my torso.

"I hate you."

He pauses, his mouth perched right above my cock. "No, you don't." He gives it a kiss and I shudder. "You hate yourself for how much you enjoy it."

He's wrong. A mouth is a mouth. I don't give a shit about who's on the other side of it. The only thing I'm interested in is getting off.

"I think you got that backward."

"Is that so?" I moan when he laps the fluid leaking from my cockhead. "Because it seems like your dick sides with me."

"Yeah, he enjoys blow jobs." I push my hips into his face. "But we both know you're enjoying it way more than he ever will… because you're obsessed with me."

I damn near whimper when he draws the tip into his mouth. "And you love it."

"Suck me already."

"You don't make the rules. I'm not doing shit until you admit how much you enjoy my attention."

"Your attention to my dick."

The tip of his tongue swirls around the small hole and I grunt. "Fuck." I look down. "Make me come."

"Not until you tell me the truth."

My nostrils flare. The price I'm forced to pay is hefty, but I need his reward. "Fine. I don't mind you sucking me off. You give great head. You're welcome to do it whenever you want."

He licks and slurps me as though my cock were a popsicle on a hot day and he's trying to prevent the juice from dripping all over him.

"Jesus." My calves clench. "Feels so fucking good."

"It will feel even better once you admit it." Wrapping his hand around my base, he runs his tongue along the underside of my shaft. "So be a good boy and tell me how much you like it."

"I like how good you suck me."

"Yeah, I know you do," he muses. "You're practically coming down my throat already." My balls throb when he dips his head and tugs each one into his mouth, releasing them with a wet pop. "You're so close."

I growl when he circles my asshole with his thumb, causing a million nerve endings to fire off at once.

"Good boys get rewarded, Cain."

My stomach drops. I know what he wants to hear. It's what started this whole fucked-up friendship in the first place. The thing I've tried not to think about…but can't ignore.

"I like your obsession with me, Damien."

I convulse when he takes my entire dick in his mouth, sucking me in deep, long pulls that make me moan and spasm until I'm shooting down his throat.

Crawling up my body, he motions for me to open my mouth. When I refuse, he plugs my nose, forcing my lips to part. I nearly gag when warm salty liquid floods my mouth and I have no choice but to swallow my own cum. Shame snakes up my spine when he shoves his tongue inside a second later, fucking my mouth as he jerks himself to the finish line.

"I know you do," he rasps before he groans, and a gush of wetness hits my sac.

I'm about to ask what he means but then he says, "Because it's awfully appealing being the object of someone's fascination." He rubs the liquid into my skin then shoves his finger in my mouth, making me taste him too. "Whether I'm touching you or not, we both know you're enjoying the view from your pedestal." His eyes bore into mine. "Otherwise you would have jumped already."

The next time he tries to kiss me, I let him.

Not because I'm attracted to him, and not because I pity him.

But because he's right.

It's nice being on someone's pedestal for once.

Chapter 23
DAMIEN

I watch as a single tear streams down her cheek. Not even her mask can hide the pain of watching the man she loves deceive her.

My muscles tighten. I can practically see the wheels in her head turning, wondering if perhaps the man walking past her isn't Cain.

After all, he too is wearing a mask.

But while Eden's mask hides her sorrow. Cain's mask hides his lies.

Hand clutching her chest, she turns, looking in the direction he left. Hoping there's been a grave mistake.

My fallen angel doesn't yet realize that while her mind tries to justify her lover's betrayal…her heart already knows the truth.

It's why that lonesome tear is making its way down her chin.

The heart is the greatest fortune teller of all time. It's always one step ahead of the curve.

Unfortunately for me—Eden's pain is something I empathize with.

Because I've experienced it myself.

Chapter 24
DAMIEN

Past...

The sound of a twig snapping outside has me opening my eyes. Turning my head toward the sound, I watch as Cain crawls through my bedroom window. Not that I'd know it was him by the looks of it. Unlike his usual polo shirts and khakis, he's sporting an oversized hoodie and sweatpants.

Other than the neon lights from my tank, it's dark in my bedroom. But from what I can see of Cain's silhouette, his hood is pulled up, and his face is pointed down toward the floor.

"Front door works just fine, man."

He says nothing.

I glance at the clock on the nightstand. It's past midnight. Cain's spent the night a few times, but he's never *arrived* here this late.

And he's certainly never crawled through my window before.

Not that I'm upset. With my dad gone for business three weeks out of the month, Cain knows he's welcome here whenever he wants. *He's the only one I bend the rules for.*

Sitting up in bed, I lean against my headboard. "What's up?"

I'm not oblivious to Cain being out of sorts, I just know he's more likely to talk if I act like everything's normal.

"Think you can get Mrs. Miller to come over?" His voice is so low I almost don't hear him.

Considering her husband gave her a black eye for not answering her phone yesterday, I doubt it.

I don't have romantic feelings for Mrs. Miller, but I do have a fondness for her. I guess you can say I consider her somewhat of a maternal figure. Which is probably all kinds of screwed up considering I've fucked her more times than I can count.

That said, I told her I'd keep the shit that goes on with her husband to myself. And unlike most people would if they knew, I don't judge her for cheating on her husband or for fucking high school students.

She's got her own demons, just like everyone else.

Reaching for my cigarettes, I bring one to my lips and light it. "Probably not. It's late."

Back turned to me, he grips the windowsill. "Is it?"

Not many things put me on edge. But Cain's recent mood swings do. I knew he was a ticking time bomb, but he should be feeling better now that I've given him an outlet for his issues.

Instead, he's unraveling a little more each day. The only time he's not is after I tie him up and get him off.

He's content after that. *Stable.* Usually hangs out in my bed with me and watches the fish…talking about anything and everything that comes to his mind.

Until he goes home, goes to school…and the cycle starts all over again.

"It's almost one in the morning."

"Oh." He blows out a shaky breath. "Is there someone else we can call? A girl who'd be down to fuck around tonight?"

I don't care that he wants to fuck a girl. Hell, I'm down to fuck a few girls tonight. But the vibe he's putting off currently doesn't sit well with me.

"I know plenty of girls, man. But before we schedule the orgy… why don't you tell me what's going on?"

He stops pacing. "Nothing. I just…I need…" His voice trails off and he bows his head.

My chest tightens as I continue staring at him. I've always been perceptive when it comes to other people's emotions. I'm not a bleeding heart by any means. Quite the contrary—I don't give a shit about most people until they give me a reason to. However, I'm sensitive to the slightest shift in their demeanor.

Probably has to do with my mother ignoring my existence. It forced me to spend a lot of time observing her and her druggie friends, which in turn made me somewhat of a people watcher.

Cain's the only one who's ever truly fascinated me though. The first time I saw him—or rather took an active interest in him—he was in a faculty room—stuffing ballots into a locked box so he could win the race for student body president.

But that wasn't what sparked the fire…it was what he did after. From my hidden spot behind a bookcase where I made Mrs. Miller give me head moments prior, I watched in amusement as Cain unzipped his pants, took out his dick, and proceeded to jerk off.

Before that incident, I'd never known anyone other than me who got a boner from doing fucked-up things. But there was Mr. Debate Team Captain himself, violently choking the chicken while he cursed Gerald Douglas—a student with special needs—to hell and back for daring to go against him in the race for student body president.

The icing on the cake was when he walked over to the fridge and jizzed inside Mrs. Douglas'—the school music teacher as well as his opponent's mother—jelly and fluff sandwich.

We might be opposites, but deep down—Cain's my kindred spirit if there ever was one.

Luckily, I knew just the right outlet for him…one that wouldn't result in the mass homicide he was clearly heading for. The guy has dreams and aspirations after all.

Unfortunately for him, it's only making him come apart at the seams.

And unfortunately for me…I seemed to have developed serious feelings for the bastard. Well, feelings other than wondering what makes him tick…and wanting to fuck his asshole so I can see if it's wound as tight as the rest of him is.

Taking a long drag off my cigarette, I study him. "Look, you're obviously going through some shit."

Silence.

I'm not the type to feed into people's dramatics, but as per fucking usual, Cain's an exception to the rule. For reasons I don't understand, he's gotten under my skin.

Rising off the bed, I walk over to him, knowing it will end in either one of two ways. With my fist in his mouth or his dick in mine as we battle it out. Either one is fine by me. Thanks to my nap I'm well rested.

I grab his shoulder. "Ca—"

He flinches and a choked sound rips from his throat as he turns. "Don't."

He's hurt, that much is evident. What I don't understand is his getup. "Why are you wearing a masquerade mask?"

From the looks of it, it's the same one I gave him two weeks ago at the dance.

When he doesn't answer, I pull it off.

My stomach turns to lead when I see his swollen black eye and split lip.

My anger is a visceral thing. Starting low in my gut and spreading outward. "I'm gonna fucking kill him."

I don't say shit like that lightly. I'm going to torture the living shit out of his father just like he's done to Cain all these years.

I go to climb out the window because it's the quickest exit, but Cain seizes my arm. "No."

"Yes." It's no longer a matter of if. It's only a matter of how fast I can get there.

He starts to open his mouth…and then—to my absolute fucking horror his eyes become glassy and he starts shaking.

"I got waitlisted." He looks at me like a child who just watched Santa kill the puppy they wished for. "They waitlisted me." He points to his chest. "Me."

Christ. I don't do well with shit like this. At all. Or maybe I do, but I wouldn't know because I don't have experience when it comes to comforting others. Fact of the matter is—I just don't care about people enough to give a shit.

But Cain's different. Because I do care. More than care…he's…I'm not sure. My neurosis? My fixation? My obsession? Perhaps all three.

All I know is he's where ninety-nine percent of my thoughts drift to as of late.

"I'm sorry, man." It's not a lie. I know getting into Harvard was important to him. "But being waitlisted isn't the end of the world, right? It's not like they turned you down."

"Being waitlisted *is* the end of the world. Do you know how many applicants they get a semester? Tons. It's their way of jerking me off so hard it burns but never letting me come."

"Interesting analogy—"

"This isn't a fucking joke, cocksucker." He starts pacing. "This is my goddamn life."

"I'm sorry." I don't know what else to say. I'm not sure there is anything else to say. "This sucks."

Nodding, he turns to face the window again. "I might as well blow my brains out and end it now."

My reaction is automatic. I grip his shoulder, much harder than before. "Don't say shit—"

"Fuck." He clutches the windowsill, his body wracking with tremors. "Don't touch me."

Harvard is the least of my worries. Ignoring his request, I reach for the hem of his sweatshirt.

It gets stuck halfway up his back and I realize it's because of all the caked-up blood sticking to the material.

If I thought my reaction was visceral before it has nothing on the storm that starts brewing inside me when I see the belt marks.

Judging from the abrasions, the motherfucker didn't use the loop. *Just the buckle.*

Running to the bathroom, I grab a few cool washcloths. Then slowly, I peel the rest of his sweatshirt off. Every inch I uncover is like my own punch to the face.

"First beating I ever felt like I deserved," Cain says, his voice cracking. "What am I gonna do, Damien?"

Before I can answer, he grips my shirt, his tears soaking the fabric. And that's how we stay for the better part of five minutes. Until he places my hand on his semi-hard dick. "I need you—"

The words are out of my mouth before he can finish his sentence. "Get on the bed. Face down."

I suck at comforting people…but this? Taking control over someone who feels out of it and blurring the lines between pain and pleasure? That *is* something I can do.

"He was so pissed," Cain says as I position myself behind him and proceed to take off his pants and boxers. "The angriest I've ever seen him in my life." He closes his eyes. "And then my brother…he just laughed and called me a loser." He scrunches his face. "He's not wrong. What kind of man lets their father beat them while their brother stands there and laughs?"

I press my lips to a wound on his tailbone. "A man who thinks he deserves it because he's been conditioned to think he does and doesn't know any better yet."

He shifts his cheek on the pillow a little to look at me. "Are you in love with me?"

That's a weird fucking question. "I'm not sure." Grabbing the washcloth I placed on the nightstand, I dab it over a wound that's still bleeding. "To be honest, I'm not sure I know how to love. I don't think I'm capable of it."

He nods. "That makes both of us." He sighs. "Promise you'll fuck Mrs. Miller for me one last time before I'm gone."

"You're not going anywhere, asshole."

"There's no point living if I can't do it the way I was supposed to."

It's not so much his words, it's the intent in his expression. Like he truly believes there's no way out other than death.

Throwing the washcloth down, I brace my arms on either side of him and lean down so I'm next to his face. "You think there's only one roadmap to your life? One way to get where you want to go?"

"For me there was."

"Then you're not half as smart as I thought you were, Mr. President."

His features harden. "Gee thanks. You and Harvard have that in common I guess."

I grit my teeth. "What I mean is, there are a hundred different paths to get to Harvard. Same goes for becoming a politician if that's really what you want. Pick one and start walking."

"It's not that easy. My dad had everything planned for me. And now that I fucked—"

"Fuck him," I shout. "Fuck your brother and Harvard too, for that matter." I grab his jaw. "There are two types of people in this world, Cain. Those who are capable of greatness, but don't bother trying. And those who still try even though they're not capable of greatness."

"But I did tr—"

"You're neither," I interject. "You're the type of person who can do anything he sets his mind to and succeed."

"You really think so?"

"You know I wouldn't say it if I didn't." I lean my forehead against his. "Everything you want is already yours. All you have to do is reach out and take it."

He draws in a breath. "I wish I could believe that, but I don't see how. My life is over."

"Your life isn't over." I run a finger down his thigh. "It's just beginning." Shifting, I plant a line of kisses down his back. "There's a reason for all the bad shit we go through, man…something that will eventually make us realize it was all worth it in the end."

He snorts. "You get that from a Hallmark card?"

"No, jackass. It's how fate works. One event leads to another… and those events lead to the next event and so on and so forth. Then one day, you look back and connect the dots. Next thing you know, everything starts making sense."

"I think Mrs. Miller's fortune teller crap is starting to rub off on you."

I bite his ass. "Yeah. Or maybe, just maybe…I'm a lot smarter than you give me credit for."

His features twist. "Harvard was everything, Damien. My father's connections are everything. There's no way I can do this without him."

I trail my lips down his ass. "Says who? Because the Cain Carter I know isn't a fucking pussy. He takes what he wants. Show your dad you can do this without him. Because you can."

His hips jerk. "I've never met anyone who believes…" He squeezes his eyes shut. "You…"

He moans when I slip my tongue between his cheeks. "Did you mean what you said before?"

I pause. "Yeah, you can do anything you—"

"No." His voice drops down a few octaves. "Did you really want to kill him for me?"

"Not did. *Do*."

"I'd never let you do that—"

I spread his cheeks and circle his asshole with my tongue.

"Fuck, that feels good." He stretches, stuffing his hands under the pillow. "But if you were going to…how would you?"

"How would I kill your father?"

He nods, arching his ass into my face.

I think about this a moment before I give him my answer. "Easy." I flick his puckered hole. "I'd make it look like an accident. Something that could never be traced back to me."

He shudders when I repeat the movement. "Jesus." Raising his ass higher, he looks up at me over his shoulder. "Like what?"

Smirking, I tease him again, this time, dipping my tongue inside. "I'd give him some sleeping pills."

His eyes go hazy. "What makes you think he'd take them?"

"Everyone eats, right? I'd find a way to put it in his food."

Groaning, I suck on the seam of his balls until he trembles.

"Then what would you do?"

Licking my finger, I push the tip of it into his hole. "I'd wait for him to fall asleep."

He bucks into my finger and my heart accelerates. "Yeah?" His voice is a deep rasp. "Then what?"

I adjust my position on the bed, lining his ass up with my dick while I continue prepping him. "Well, before the pills, I would have re-wired an everyday household item...something simple…maybe a coffee maker or toaster. This way, they'd blame it on faulty wiring."

"Blame what on faulty wiring?"

Slipping my finger out, I grab some lube on the nightstand and give my cock a languid stroke. "The fire that would kill him."

Cain's breathing hitches as I proceed to work my dick between his cheeks. "Why a fire?"

I groan when a pearlescent drop lands directly on his puckered hole. "Because they don't leave much evidence behind…especially if you do it in the middle of the night. People are sleeping, so the neighbors are less likely to call the fire department, therefore there would be more damage. More damage usually equals less evidence." I swirl my tip around the liquid, slowly working my cock-head in. "And since he'd be full of sleeping pills…he'd never make it out alive. Not unless someone tried to rescue him."

Cain clenches the sheet in his hand, gasping for air. "Oh, fuck."

"Relax, man. It will only hurt for a little while." With a grunt, I push my hips forward, watching my wide crown disappear inside him. The sensation feels so good, it's all I can do not to come on the spot.

"Don't worry, I'm gonna take care of you."

His body goes slack, and when I look down, I notice a large wet spot underneath him.

He already came.

~

Cain isn't next to me when I wake up the next morning.

When I call his cell to see where he went, he tells me he'll see me at school later.

Which is why I think nothing of it when I catch him in the locker room after seventh period rummaging around for something in his locker. His back is to me, but I notice he's donning his usual polo shirt and khakis.

I run a finger up his arm. "How are you feeling?"

He tenses. "Fine."

On one hand, I'm happy he's back to normal. On the other, I'm worried he's back to normal. It will just empower his father to do it again.

"Back to business as usual then, huh?"

"Uh, yeah. Sure."

Looking around to make sure we're alone, I take a step closer to him. "I told Kristy not to come tonight. Figured you should take the night off." I close the distance between us and my hand slowly makes its way to the front of his pants. "You can still come over and—"

An elbow to my stomach makes my head whirl. "What the f—"

"What the fuck is right."

I can feel the color drain from my face. No black eye or split lip. *He's not Cain.*

"Man, I heard you were a freak but—" He stops mid-sentence, his face lighting up. "Holy shit." He starts laughing as he looks between me and the locker. "You thought I was my brother, didn't you? This is…wow. I knew he was spending time with a buddy lately, but I didn't think it was *that* kind of buddy." He laughs harder. "Wait until my dad hears about—"

My hand is around his throat before he can finish that sentence. "Listen to me, you sick fuck. Whatever's going through that perverted head of yours is wrong."

"Really? Because it sounds like you and my brother are—"

"Hanging out with girls and partying? Christ, I know you're a nerd, but it's nothing to get your panties in a twist over."

"Wait, he's been partying with *you* lately?"

Removing my hand from his throat, I pull a bag of weed out of my pocket. "Yeah, sometimes we get really freaky and smoke the devil's lettuce. Which is what I was trying to discreetly slip you—or rather, your brother—before. My dad just paid a shit ton of money to clear up my last incident, I don't need to cop another. Know what I mean?"

He nods. "Yeah. I mean no, but yeah. Makes sense." He rubs his neck. "Didn't mean to insinuate you were a faggot. My bad."

Too bad I'm a long way from done. He's not leaving this locker room without me fucking up his perfect life. I consider it foreplay for the ass-kicking I'm going to give him when he least expects it.

I smirk as I recall who his girlfriend is. "By the way—tell Kim I said hi." I lean in like I'm about to tell him a secret. "Between me and you, her halitosis combined with that hairy mole on her face is off-putting, but if you give her a mint and close your eyes…her blow jobs aren't all that bad." I fix his collar. "Then again, why am I telling you this? I'm sure you already know."

"Kimmy would never fuck you," he deadpans. "She's loyal to me."

He's going to make a great politician. He's so convincing, I almost believe the words out of his mouth.

Unfortunately for him, *Kimmy* isn't as loyal as she pretends to be.

And unfortunately for Kimmy, she fucked someone with a near photographic memory who pays attention to details.

"She's got a birthmark shaped like Alaska on her ass. Her nipples are a deep rosy pink. Around the size of half-dollar coins, probably the most attractive thing about her." I rub my forehead. "There's something else…oh, that's right. I popped her cherry back in…" I snap my fingers. "February. In the library. Fiction section. She's a huge Jane Austen fan." I roll my eyes. "Then again, aren't they all?"

His jaw drops. He honestly looks so hurt it's downright hysterical.

I wince. "Ouch. She probably told you it was a tampon or bicycle incident, huh?" I blow out a breath. "Damn. These hoes just ain't loyal after all."

His jaw tics. "That fucking bitch."

"Yeah, man," I say as he rushes past me. "You go let her have it."

Slipping my phone out of my pocket, I shoot Cain a text.

Damien: Weird incident with your brother in the locker room today. Long story short, I thought he was you. Don't worry, I covered. But if he brings it up when you see him, go with the flow. We party and fuck girls.

Chapter 25
CAIN

Past...

"I knew that asshole was lying," my brother sneers, holding up the phone Damien gave me. "Kim's gonna feel like an idiot at school tomorrow when I tell everyone she cheated on me with a homo."

I laugh—not because he's right. But because he won't be at school tomorrow.

"Why the fuck are you laughing?" An evil grin spreads across his face. "Won't be so funny once I tell dad his son's a faggot." He snorts. "Christ, I should have eaten you in the womb."

I slip a pair of gloves on as he strides toward the door. "Dad's sleeping."

Walking up behind him, I pull the plastic bag out of my pocket and raise it over my head. He didn't want the milkshake I made him, so it's on to plan B. "He said he had a long day and wanted to get some shuteye."

When he starts to turn, I dive into action, slipping the bag over his head and then tackling him to the ground.

He writhes and thrashes, trying his hardest to get the bag off his head. Poor guy even manages to make a small tear in the first one. However, I was one step ahead and made sure to triple bag it. Can't have him gaining leverage on me. Or worse, escaping and running to the neighbors.

I lock my legs around his waist when his flailing gets worse. "It will be more peaceful for us both if you stop struggling."

After what feels like an eternity, his movements stop altogether.

Taking the bag off his head, I stuff it in the pocket of my hoodie, making a mental note to get rid of it on my way to Damien's house later.

Then I haul him onto his bed since that's where I need him to be.

A shiver goes up my spine. It's eerie seeing your identical twin dead. Like a disturbing glimpse into the future.

Guess Mrs. Miller's tarot cards were right after all.

Smirking, I blow a kiss to his corpse. "So long, brother. Looks like a spot just opened up after all. I'll be sure to make the most of my time at Harvard."

Chapter 26
DAMIEN

Past...

A hand slithering up my thigh has me bolting up in bed.

"Cain?"

He's hovering over me, wearing the same black hoodie and sweatpants from last night. Shaking like a goddamn leaf.

"What's—"

I can't even get the words out before he attacks me with his mouth and squeezes my now thickening cock through my boxers.

To say I'm surprised would be an understatement. Cain might be the instigator, but I'm the initiator when it comes to our hookups.

I can't recall a single time he's ever touched my junk.

He groans into my mouth, but I don't return the sentiment. His kiss is equal parts sloppy and frantic...it's different. Doesn't feel right.

I pull away. "What's going on with you?"

"Nothing." He tugs on my boxers and my cock springs free. "I'm just checking out the equipment under the hood."

"Are you drunk?"

He whistles. "Damn. You're even bigger than I am. No wonder everyone's always on your dick."

I quirk a brow. "High?"

"Stone cold sober." Wrapping his hand around my length, he gives me a firm stroke. "Christ, I can't believe I let you put this in my ass last night."

"You didn't." I give him a smirk. "Just the tip."

His eyes darken. "I liked it." Another stroke. "I'm becoming fond of this, too."

I eye him suspiciously. "That's funny. Last I remember—the only part you were fond of was getting off."

His lips twitch. "Well, a mouth's a mouth, right?" He climbs on the bed and kneels between my legs. "And I know exactly where I want mine right now."

Faster than I can blink, he lowers his head and swipes his tongue over my cockhead. It's so quick that for a moment, I think I imagined it.

He looks up. "You like that?"

I press my thumb into his bottom lip. I've been with hundreds of girls and he's got the nicest pair of lips I've ever encountered. They're full and pouty, like two soft pillows on his face. "I've been wondering what these lips would feel like wrapped around me since the dance. Why don't you show me?"

He hesitates before flicking the liquid leaking from my tip.

Fisting my dick, I hold it out to him. "I don't like cock teasers. If you're gonna walk into my bedroom with the intention of sucking me off, you better do it right."

Leaning in, he takes my entire crown into his mouth.

I grin. "You're getting warmer."

My cock jerks as he glides down my shaft. "That feels go—"

A groan rips from my throat as he starts sucking me hard and fast. "Jesus." His movements speed up and I clutch the nightstand. "That's it, suck me just like that."

His head continues bobbing up and down and gagging sounds

fill the room. If I had any doubt Cain wanted my dick before, I don't anymore.

My hand finds the back of his head, keeping him there. "Relax your mouth so I can fuck it for a little while."

He stills, and I thrust my hips, hitting the back of his throat. "You like my dick in your mouth?" He nods, and I thrust harder, making him choke on it.

Until I can't take it anymore.

I tug on his hair until he releases me. "I want your ass."

That's the only warning he gets before I slam him belly down on the mattress and pull off his pants, revealing his stark white behind.

Grabbing some lube from the nightstand, I pour it on two of my fingers before I plunge them between his cheeks, prepping him.

He grips the sheets as I proceed to work the head of my dick in next. "This might hurt."

He barely has time to give me a nod before I'm pushing my hips forward, ramming my entire cock inside him.

"Fuck," he chokes out as I pull back and slam into him again.

My balls ache as I feel him stretch around me, taking every inch I give him. They downright sizzle when I hear him groan my name.

"You like the way I'm fucking your tight little ass, huh?"

"Yes." He hisses when I swivel my pelvis, grinding into him. "Harder."

Pinning his arms to the bed, I cover his body with mine and pick up the pace, plowing him so hard into the mattress my goddamn teeth rattle.

"I'm close."

I pull him upright, making him sit on it, then spit into my hand and start jerking him.

Sputtering a curse, he drives into my palm and I match his thrusts.

"Jesus fucking Christ." My climax is powerful, whipping through me like a twister as I empty every drop inside his asshole.

A moment later he convulses and spurts all over my hand.

We're both breathless as my release trickles out of him and onto my softening cock.

Bringing my hand to my mouth, I lick up his cum, then reach for my cigarettes.

I light one for me and one for him before I settle against the headboard.

I'm nice and relaxed, Cain however; starts trembling.

Fuck. I exhale deeply, preparing to give him the ol' *it's okay, everyone experiments* speech. "Look, taking a dick every once in—"

"Do you love me?"

Evidently, I had nothing to worry about because Cain sounds like he's ready to walk down the aisle.

I start to give him the same answer I did last night, but stop and seriously consider his question.

They say there are some people you're inexplicably drawn to… people who are meant to change your life in some profound way.

However, I'd never met anyone who felt like they were part of my destiny before. I was a lone wolf.

Until Cain.

And just because I'm not capable of feeling rainbows and butterflies doesn't mean what I feel for him isn't love. Maybe my fixation with Cain *is* my version of love?

"Yes." I take a long drag of my cigarette. "Does that scare you?"

"No." He shifts on the bed, facing me. "I have bigger things to be scared of right now."

"Like what?"

His face goes blank, devoid of any emotion. "I'm in serious deep shit."

"If this is about Harvard—"

"It's not." He looks at me. "It's so much bigger than that."

I tap my skull with my knuckles. "This thing works, but I'm gonna need you to spell it out for me, man. What's going—"

He collapses against me, his body wracking with tremors. *Shit.*

I'm at a total loss of what to do. "Cain—"

"I did something, Damien," he whispers. "Something really

bad. Something that could ruin my entire life if anyone ever finds out."

My stomach sinks like a stone. "I've got your back. Whatever it is, you can tell me, and I'll figure out a way to fix it."

"You can't fix this."

The pit forming in my stomach widens along with the ominous feeling snaking up my spine. "Cain—"

The sound of a phone ringing cuts me off.

"That's mine."

I watch as he gets off the bed, cool as a cucumber.

"Hello," he answers with a sleepy voice.

I look at the clock on the nightstand. It's just after three in the morning.

I assume it's his father, until he says, "Speaking. Who's this?"

The cigarette I was about to light stops halfway to my lips as my ears tune in.

"What," Cain shouts. "How? No. You're lying. Oh, God."

I leap from the bed, ready to pummel whoever's on the other end of that phone.

"This can't be happening." He clutches his stomach. "Please tell me this is a horrible mistake." His voice cracks. "No. I spent the night at a friend's house." He starts sobbing and my chest knots. "I turned eighteen last month, but I'll give my grandmother a call." He presses the heel of his palm to his forehead. "She lives in a different state." Another tear falls down his cheek. "I won't. I'll ask my friend. I'll be there shortly."

"What happened?"

He wipes his eyes. "I'm gonna need a ride to the hospital."

"No problem." I stare at him when he starts getting dressed. "Are you gonna tell me what happened?"

He spins around. "Oh, right." His expression turns to stone. "My father and brother died." His dark eyes cut to mine. "House fire."

Chapter 27
CAIN

Past...

"I'm sorry, what?" Under the table, I wipe my sweaty palms on my pants. "What does that mean?"

It's been a little over forty-eight hours since the fire, and early this morning I received a phone call asking me to come down to the local precinct. I wasn't nervous...until now.

Detective Trejo steeples his hands and places them on the table. He went to high school with my dad and they stayed friends throughout the years, so I know the loss is hitting him hard. Unfortunately for me, it means he's personally invested in the case.

"Son," he says slowly, like I'm a goddamn idiot. "When people perish in a fire, there are certain things you expect to find in regards to the body. Your father, for instance, had soot in his throat and lungs. He was also found crouched on the floor of his bedroom facing the door, which indicates he was trying to escape when he passed."

My expression changes to one of anguish. "Why didn't he jump out the window?" I rub my forehead, forcing myself to breathe. "I'm sorry. I didn't...it's just..."

He holds up a hand. "It's all right. Anger is part of grieving. And to answer your question, it's most likely because the house was already engulfed in flames by the time he woke up, making it impossible to see a path to safety." He frowns. "The autopsy report showed traces of an over the counter sleeping pill. Not enough to cause damage, but more than the standard amount recommended. That combined with the fire would result in him being highly disoriented."

Blowing out a breath, I look up at the ceiling. "He mentioned he was stressed with work and having trouble sleeping during dinner that night. I didn't think anything of it at the time, but if I did maybe he'd still be here."

He holds up a hand. "Your father wouldn't want you to blame yourself. There's no way you could have known what was going to happen."

Gripping the back of my neck, I look down at the table. "Right." My brows furrow. "Sorry, you were trying to tell me something important about my brother before. What was it?"

"Ah, yes." He folds his hands on the table again. "The autopsy determined your father was killed during the fire. Caleb's death, however, is a different story."

I blink. "How so?"

"There were no traces of soot in his throat or lungs, and his carbon dioxide levels were inconsistent with those who die in fires. Also, the position he was found in was…abnormal given the nature of the situation."

My palms begin to sweat again. "Abnormal how?"

"He was found lying in a supine position on his bed. Granted, your brother's room was farthest from where the fire started in the kitchen, but he still suffered some exterior burns." He gives me a solemn look. "Cain, what I'm about to tell you is serious."

My heart is pounding so fast I'm surprised he can't hear it from where he's sitting. "I'm listening."

He puts down his pen. "Given the unusual findings, the medical examiner is confident your brother did not die in the fire…but before it. There were signs—for instance, his bloodshot eyes—that give him reason to believe Caleb was intentionally suffocated and the fire was staged as a coverup."

"Wait, you're saying someone *killed* my brother?"

"That's exactly what I'm saying. And the only way we're going to get to the bottom of this is if you're completely honest with me. Understand?"

I nod.

He places his notepad in front of him. "Does Caleb have any enemies? Someone he doesn't get along with?"

My mouth goes dry. "No, none that I can think of. Everyone loved him. He was awesome."

"Cain."

"Yes?"

"I know it's hard, but I really need you to think."

"I'm telling you the truth, Detective. Caleb didn't have any enemies."

He runs his finger over his lips. "What about you?"

"What about me?"

"He's your identical twin. Perhaps someone holding a grudge against you thought he was you."

"I thought you said he was in his bedroom? We have separate bedrooms. Why would someone think he was me?"

He shrugs. "Maybe someone broke in without knowing the layout of the house."

"Wouldn't that be risky?" I take a shallow breath. "Not to be disrespectful, but if someone is going to commit such a heinous act, you would assume they'd take the proper measures to ensure they wouldn't get caught."

His eyes narrow. "I've been working homicide for over fifteen years, Cain. Trust me when I tell you…every murderer leaves a clue behind. And it's up to people like me to find it." He sits up straight. "Can you think of anyone who might want to harm you?"

"No. I don't have any enemies either. I mean, my ex-girlfriend isn't too fond of me right now, but she'd never harm me. Plus, she

knows exactly where my bedroom is, so she'd never mistake me—"
My eyes widen. "Shit."

The detective practically hops over the table. "What?"

"Nothing." I close my eyes. "It's nothing."

"Cain, if you know something—"

"I made a promise to my brother and I'm not breaking it."

"Your silence does him no good if it could solve his murder."

"But I promised him I wouldn't tell a soul." I trace an invisible pattern on the table with my finger. "If something like this got out it could ruin people's lives."

"People's lives are already ruined. Your silence only ensures it will ruin more."

I look around the room. "Can I have some water?"

Walking over to the small desk in the corner, he picks up a pitcher and a paper cup, then places them in front of me.

I take my time filling it. I want him on the edge of his seat, waiting for me to drop this nugget on his lap.

"Before I tell you, can you assure me it will stay between us? It's just…Caleb had a good reputation in the community. I don't want to destroy it."

"I understand. I assure you whatever you tell me won't be made public knowledge. Unless it leads to an arrest, in which case I can't guarantee certain details won't get out."

"I don't think that will be the case. But you said if I knew something to tell you, right?"

"Right."

"Caleb was involved with a teacher at our school."

"Involved in what manner?"

I give him a look. "The inappropriate kind."

He presses his pen to the pad. "What's her name?"

"Mrs. Miller. I don't know her first name, but she teaches—"

"Science over at the high school."

"Yeah, and her husband is an assistant football coach."

"I know. He does some electrical work—" He clears his throat and I can practically see the wheels in his head turning. "Sorry, go on."

"Mrs. Miller and Caleb were involved for a little while. Things between them were getting…intense. To be frank, he was in over his head. And she…" My sentence trails off and I look away.

"She what?"

My jaw tics. "She kept dangling the carrot in front of his face. She'd end things one week…only to lead him on the next. It was making him a little mental, to be honest. Especially when Caleb found out he wasn't the only student she was screwing."

Detective Trejo nearly spits out his coffee. "Oh?"

I nod. "Yeah. My father warned us about getting caught up with women like that, but Caleb didn't listen." I shrug. "Can't really blame him, she is beautiful."

"Beauty doesn't absolve someone of their offenses. Please continue."

"The other student she was messing with…he's my friend. That's how I found out."

"What's your friend's name?"

"Damien King."

He makes a noise in the back of his throat as he writes down his name on the pad. "How did your brother react when he found out?"

I wince. "He was pissed. Not at Damien, because they were friends too, but Mrs. Miller. He told me her sleeping with another student was the equivalent of her cheating on him."

He raises a brow. "But she's married."

I slap the table. "I know. That's exactly what I said." I sigh heavily. "This is the part I'm scared to tell you about…it doesn't paint him in a positive light."

"No matter what your brother did, he is still the victim in this situation. However, I can't help him if you don't tell me everything."

"You're right." I drum my nails on the desk. "He didn't take the news well. He threatened to tell her husband about her affairs if she didn't divorce him by the time Caleb graduated." I roll my eyes. "I tried to talk some sense into him, but he was convinced everything would be perfect if she left her husband. He was so obsessed with her, he didn't realize she was only using him." My stomach clenches. "I think she liked all the attention he gave her, probably made her feel special."

"I see." He puts his pen back down. "Do you know when your brother first became involved with her?"

I shake my head. "No, not exactly. I only found out about them last month during his—our—eighteenth birthday. She came over in the middle of the night and I ended up walking in on them while they were…you know…in his bedroom." I screw up my face, pretending to think. "If I had to take a guess, I'd say about three months or so. That's when he started acting a little weird. Like he was hiding something."

"So your brother was a minor?"

"Look, Detective. I know what you're getting at, but I'm not looking to get her in trouble. I don't like that she led my brother on, but he was a very willing participant." I hitch a shoulder up. "She's actually kind of cool. She was the fortune teller at the spring fling two weeks ago and did a reading on me and my date, Julia. Julia loved it and—"

A knock on the door cuts me off mid-sentence. "Sorry to interrupt," a voice behind me says. "This is important."

Detective Trejo rises from his seat. "Excuse me, Cain. I'll be back shortly."

With that, he walks out.

Placing my head in my hands, I exhale heavily, blinking back tears. I'm not stupid, this might not be an official interrogation, but I know every move I make is being watched and scrutinized whether a detective is in here with me or not. And right now? I'm supposed to be grieving my losses.

About fifteen minutes later Detective Trejo walks back in. I'm not sure what to make of the look on his face.

"I'm going to need to keep you here a little while longer." He sits down on the seat across from me. "There's been a crack in the case."

My blood pressure rises, but I force myself to remain calm. "What happened?"

I can see him mulling something over in his head before he speaks. "You mentioned Mrs. Miller was a fortune teller at your high school dance, correct?"

"Yeah, like I said, she gave me and my date a reading." I raise a brow. "Why?"

He rubs his chin. "Did she use tarot cards by any chance?"

"She did actually. She said they belonged to her grandmother who used to do it for a living." I make a face. "But I don't understand what any of that has to do with the fire and Caleb's death."

"The investigators found something unusual—or rather—two unusual things under Caleb's pillow."

"Like what?"

"From what they can tell it's a pair of women's underwear…and what appears to be a tarot card."

Chapter 28
DAMIEN

Past…

A hand cupping my balls makes me wake with a jolt. When I open my eyes, Cain's looking down at me, smiling. "Hey, buddy. Long time no see."

Pushing his hand away, I swing my legs over the bed and sit up. "Where have you been?"

It's been forty-eight hours since I last saw or heard from him … and today, Mrs. Miller was arrested at school.

At first, I thought it was because of her fondness for fucking students, but whispers started circulating that she's been charged with Caleb's murder.

Which doesn't make any fucking sense. At all.

Cain starts walking around the room, idly touching my things. "Sorry, I've been a little busy talking to investigators and planning a double funeral." He gives me a lopsided smile. "Looks like your stalker skills are getting rusty." He saunters toward the bed. "I think you liked me better when you couldn't have me."

I reach for my cigarettes and light one. "I liked you better when you were honest with me."

He takes the cigarette from my lips and takes a drag. "What makes you think I'm not being honest with you?"

I snatch it back from him. "Mrs. Miller was arrested today." He goes for the string on my sweatpants, but I swat his hand away. "Did you hear what I said?"

He drops to his knees before me. "Does that upset you?"

"It doesn't make me happy. People are saying she was arrested for your brother's murder."

He plants a line of open-mouth kisses down my abs. "I know." My dick stirs as he ventures lower. "Such a shame." There's a twinkle in his eye as he looks up at me. "I had no idea she was fucking my brother, too. That would have made for some real kinky shit. Talk about a missed opportunity."

I bite my lip when he nips my thigh through my sweatpants. "We both know she wasn't fucking him. And she definitely didn't kill him."

My cock twitches when his mouth slides along the outline of my hardening dick. "Are you sure? Because according to Detective Trejo, the DNA on the pair of panties found under his pillow matched hers...and the tarot card came from her deck." He unties the string to my sweatpants. "They think she crawled into his bed, seduced him, and then when he least expected it...suffocated him with a pillow."

I raise an eyebrow. "And then mysteriously caused a short circuit that led to a fire?"

He pulls on the elastic and my cock springs out, oblivious to the severity of the conversation.

"I mean, she is a science teacher after all. Not to mention, her husband's an electrician. I'm sure he taught her a few things." He kisses my tip and edges back slightly. My balls twitch when I see the string of pre-cum connecting us before he licks it away. "Kind of like how you taught me a few things."

"Cain." I wait for him to look at me. "Lie to everyone else, but don't lie to me."

He closes his eyes and sighs. "Look, I panicked, okay? The only way to save *you* was to throw *her* under the bus in the interrogation room."

I'm about to point out that he planted her panties and the card underneath Caleb's pillow *before* he was ever interrogated, but I'm too caught off guard by his statement.

"Save me? They thought I did it?"

Cain gives me a languid stroke. "I don't know, but when I mentioned I stayed at your house the night of the fire and you were my alibi, the detective kept grilling me about you." He plants a line of kisses up and down my shaft. "I know you don't have a great history with the local police department, and I wanted to protect you…as well as myself. However, the only way to do that was to divert their attention to someone else."

"Why Mrs. Miller?"

He shrugs. "The police are more likely to think someone's guilty if they have a track record of doing shady things. Hence why they were looking at *you*. However, a teacher cheating on her husband with multiple students is way shadier than a teenager with drugs. Don't you think?"

"There are plenty of corrupt people in this town," I remind him. "I don't see why you had to pin it on an innocent woman who gets beat on by her husband."

Cain scowls. "I'm sorry, I didn't realize you were in love with her and you'd rather her stay out of jail than me."

He starts to get up, but I haul him back down. "You know I'm on your side no matter what. I'm just trying to wrap my head around what's happening."

Smirking, his eyes drop to my dick. "Me too." He laps the vein on the underside of my shaft. "I'm sorry about Mrs. Miller, but it was the only way." He shoves me so I'm lying down. "Let me make it up to you."

My hand goes to his hair, gripping the short strands as he works me slowly, drawing out my pleasure.

Cain might be wrong for what he did, but I get it. We're two sides of the same coin after all. That's part of the draw between us. No one in the world will get me like he does and vice versa.

Cain throwing Mrs. Miller to the wolves was nothing personal. He needed a fall guy, and unfortunately for her, she was it. Had he told me *he* was going to murder his abusive father and brother, I'd have steered him toward a different target to pin it on—but that's not how it played out.

The only thing I can do now is protect the both of us.

"They're probably gonna want to talk to me at some point," I say as I watch his head bob up and down. "Mind filling me in on what you said so our stories match?"

He releases me with a wet pop. "I told Detective Trejo, Mrs. Miller was sleeping with Caleb and he became obsessed with her." He tongues my cockhead. "And when he found out she was sleeping with another student, he lost it and threatened to tell her husband." He winks. "Thus, giving her motive."

I look down the length of my body at him. "Did you mention the student's name?"

"No." His mouth drops to my balls and I suppress a groan. "But they're probably going through her phone records as we speak, so prepare yourself to get called in." His teeth graze my length and I hiss. "Don't worry, though. I told the detective you and Caleb were friends and he wasn't mad at you. He was mad at her for being a stupid whore."

"She's not a stupid whore. She's just a person who doesn't always make the right choices. She's human."

So is Cain.

And deep down, no matter how good we think we are…we're all a little evil inside.

The devil was once an angel. Not the other way around.

"Look, I know you liked her, but Mrs. Miller isn't the only woman in the world to take your mommy issues out on. There are plenty of other Mrs. Miller's we can fuck," he says between long sucks. "But even if there weren't, you'll always have me. I'll take good care of you, Damien." I roll my hips when the tip of his tongue finds the sensitive spot between my sac and ass. "I'll stay perched on my pedestal looking down on you. I'll never ignore you like she did."

I moan his name as he continues working me to the finish line, the organ in my chest hammering like a drum.

My feelings for Cain aren't wrong. We both might do shitty things and we're not good people…but we're in whatever this thing is together.

Cain's more than someone I fuck. He's more than my best friend.

He's more than my fixation.

He's the person who was meant to change my life…because he already has.

Chapter 29
DAMIEN

Past...

I grit my teeth. "I was eighteen the first time we had sex. But even if I wasn't, it wouldn't matter. The age of consent in this state is seventeen. And trust me, I consented. Therefore, this little interrogation of yours is useless."

Detective Trejo sighs. "It's not useless. Your teacher is being charged with the murder of a student she had sexual relations with. You are *also* a student she had sexual relations with and most importantly, a friend of the victim. You can give us the information we need to help us understand what happened to your friend, Damien."

My hands clench at my sides. I have Cain's back, but it doesn't mean I like the idea of sending Mrs. Miller further down the river. She didn't deserve to be arrested in the middle of classes two days ago and she sure as shit doesn't deserve to be sitting in a jail cell right now.

But it's either her or Cain.

And I'll always choose Cain. I'd do anything in the world for him.

Including going along with his ridiculous story that frames an innocent woman for a murder she didn't commit, but *he* did.

However, I'm not throwing Mrs. Miller under the bus completely. I'm going to stick to Cain's story…but I'm going to plant some breadcrumbs of my own and steer them in another direction.

And if everything works out in the end, I'll make someone else pay for Caleb's murder.

Someone who deserves to suffer for their sins.

I glare at him. "Sorry, Detective, but I don't keep a ledger on the women I fuck. I barely even remember their names."

He gives me a smug smile. "Lucky for you, I have that information handy. Now, can you recall how many times you had sex with your teacher, Mrs. Kristy Miller?"

"I don't know." I smirk, sizing him up. "If I had to take a gander, I'd say…a lot more than you and your wife."

He slams his hand on the table. "Listen to me, punk. You think your shit doesn't stink, but I will toss your ass in a cell the next time you mouth off."

I lean forward. "And my father will bail me out before the end of the day." I look around. "In fact, maybe I should call him and tell him I need a lawyer—"

"No." He straightens in his seat. It's hysterical how much officers hate lawyers getting involved with their interrogations. Especially the kind of lawyers my father has access to. They eat officers like him for breakfast. "That's not necessary. For once, you're not in any trouble. I just need you to answer a few questions." He takes a sip of his coffee. "I think we got off on the wrong foot, so let's try this again, shall we?"

Before I can retort, he clicks his pen. "Can you recall how long you've been having sexual relations with your teacher?"

Since the first day of classes. "I don't know, a few weeks."

"Did you ever have sex on school property?"

"What does that have to do with Caleb's murder?"

"Answer the question."

"No, we never had sex on school property."

His eyes become tiny slits. "Dami—"

"Once or twice in a storage closet, okay?"

He jots something down on his notepad. "Did you ever exchange telephone calls, texts, or emails with her?"

"Nope."

Smoke is practically coming out of his ears. "I can petition a court for your phone records."

"Why would you bother doing that? Last time I checked, phones work both ways. Therefore, you already have a record of every text and phone call between us. You say you want me to help you get to the bottom of Caleb's murder, yet you're wasting our time asking me questions you already know the answers to."

"Why are you being so difficult?" He jabs a finger into the table. "In my experience, people are only hostile when they're guilty of something." He stands. "Is that it? Is the guilt finally settling in and making you lash out, Damien?"

"No, because I have nothing to feel guilty about."

"Are you sure? Because according to Mrs. Miller's phone records, you two have been sexually involved for quite some time. A *lot* longer than a few weeks and a lot longer than she and Caleb have." He starts circling me. "Caleb's brother claims you were friends, but you know what I think?"

"I don't really care."

He gets so close to my face I can smell the coffee on his breath. "Well, you should care because *I* think you were jealous that your friend started having sex with the teacher you fell in love with. Jealous enough to kill him. Stupid enough to try and make it look like an accident. And bitter enough to set up the woman who hurt you to take the fall for it."

"Wow, that's quite the story there, Detective. There's just one problem with your theory."

"What's that?"

"Cain was sleeping at my house the night of the fire. We were up the whole night drinking and playing video games. I'm pretty sure he would remember me leaving *my* house to set fire to his."

His jaw works. "Fine. If my story isn't what really happened, tell me what did."

"How am I supposed to know?"

With a grunt, he starts circling the room again. "According to Mrs. Miller, she never slept with Caleb. She said she slept with you and *Cain*. She also said you both liked to tie her up and would participate in sexual acts together. All three of you. So *that*, Damien King, tells me you know quite a bit more than you're claiming you do."

Shit.

He pauses behind me. "And you know, I didn't want to believe her. I really didn't. But then you come in here with your smug attitude refusing to answer questions that could clear some of this up. And suddenly? She starts looking innocent. And you and Cain start looking really guilty." He leans down. "Especially since there is no record of her ever talking to Caleb on the phone. Yet, you and Cain keep insisting she was sexually involved with *him*. Why is that?"

"Because she was."

I take a deep breath. I was ready for this. I'm known for giving the local police a hard time, and if I walked in here too friendly today, he'd know something was off.

But if I let him think he cracked me open, and I'm finally starting to cooperate because I have no other choice, he'll feel like he won the golden ticket.

"I think I need a lawyer."

"You don't need a lawyer if you tell me the truth."

"If I tell you the truth, Caleb's reputation is destroyed, and I don't think that's fair to do to him since he's no longer here to defend it."

"You don't strike me as the kind of guy to care about someone else's reputation."

"You're right. I'm not." I pull my old phone—the one I gave to

Cain—out of my pocket—and the current one I use. "But Caleb is. He never used his phone to talk to her. He used mine."

"There are two phones on the table."

"I know. Caleb didn't want anything being traced back to him." The best lie is the one closest to the truth. "Not only did he get accepted to Harvard and was on his way up the political ladder, but he had a girlfriend. He didn't want her to know he was cheating on her. So, in the spirit of friendship, I gave him my old phone and told him to use it to talk to Mrs. Miller and whoever else he wanted to. I got myself a new one."

"So, Mrs. Miller was right. The three of you were sexually involved."

"We messed around with her together, yes." I grin. "I'll leave the explicit details up to your imagination."

He sits back down in the seat across from me. "It didn't bother you to watch him have sex with the same woman you were having sex with?"

"Hell no." I lick my lips. "I enjoy watching the people I fuck, fuck other people…while I fuck their brains out." I flash him some teeth. "However, that's where all the excitement ends for me. I didn't get emotionally attached to her like Caleb did. Relationships aren't really my thing. Never have been."

His forehead wrinkles. "According to his brother, Caleb became jealous when he found out you two were involved. Yet, you're saying he was comfortable *watching* you sleep with her."

"I'm not sure why Cain would say that when Caleb's jealousy was directed toward Mrs. Miller's husband." I swallow. "But you'd be surprised what someone would do…what rules they would break for the person they're infatuated with." I clear my throat. "Anyway, Caleb probably never told Cain about it because he didn't want his brother to know he was having threesomes with a guy. Not everyone is a free spirit when it comes to sex, and most people aren't comfortable talking about their sex life with their family members."

He brings his pen to his lips. "Thank you for your insight. However, there's still one more thing that doesn't quite add up."

"What's that?"

"Why is Mrs. Miller insisting that she was sleeping with Cain… not Caleb?"

I smirk. "Come on, Detective. You're a smart man. Caleb and Cain are *identical* twins. Why would she admit to sleeping with Caleb when she can claim she slept with Cain? In other words—the twin she's *not* being accused of murdering."

He blinks rapidly as though the thought never occurred to him before he furiously jots something down on his notepad.

"And earlier when you said Caleb got emotionally attached, you mean—"

"Obsessed. Mrs. Miller was all he would talk about. Her leaving her husband consumed his every waking thought."

"Did Caleb ever threaten to harm Mrs. Miller?"

"Not unless she asked for it." I wince, preparing to steer this boat in another direction. "Her husband, the part-time *electrician*, on the other hand…"

He stops writing. "What about her husband?"

"Let's just say Mrs. Miller was into rough sex with me and Caleb because she liked to turn all the pain her bastard husband caused her into pleasure."

"Her husband hits her?"

"Hits. Punches. Chokes. Sometimes all three."

"Did you ever urge her to report him to the authorities?"

"She's a twenty-nine-year-old woman with a degree, Detective. She knows she can report him if she wanted to. She, like most people in her situation, fear the repercussions."

His gaze turns scrutinizing. "And yet she found the time to cheat on her husband regularly. Most women in abusive situations are far too scared to do something like that." The judgment in his tone is apparent. "Not to mention, her husband took out a second mortgage and a loan to pay for her bail at the courthouse this morning. Doesn't sound like someone who would want to har—" The sound of his phone ringing cuts him off mid-sentence. "Excuse me, I have to take this."

I start to stand up, but he points to the chair and mouths, "Sit."

Reluctantly I plop back down.

"What?" he exclaims, dropping his pen. "When?" He turns ashen. "I see. I'll be there shortly."

A strange feeling claws up my spine as he hangs up the phone and stands.

"You're free to go."

I stay rooted to my seat. "Why? What happened?"

His pompous expression from before is now one of sorrow. "It seems you were right."

My stomach twists and my chest becomes heavy.

I already know the next words out of his mouth before he says them.

"Shortly after they arrived home from the courthouse, Mrs. Miller's husband beat her to death, and then shot himself."

"Congratulations, Detective," I bite as I walk toward the door. "You were so busy blaming her for a murder she didn't commit, and questioning me about my sex life, the real killer got away with it."

Chapter 30
DAMIEN

Past...

"Did you speak to Detective Trejo?"

"Jesus Christ." My heart rate accelerates at the sound of Cain's voice in the pitch-black room. "Give me a heads-up next time."

My eyes adjust, and I see the desk chair Cain's sitting on shift slightly, but he doesn't turn around. He keeps his focus glued to the tank—which is weird as fuck given the neon lights are turned off.

Then again, Cain's not exactly normal. *Neither of us are.*

We're two screwed up peas in one fucked-up pod.

Which is why I can't blame him for what happened to Mrs. Miller.

If the roles were reversed—I might have sacrificed someone Cain cared about in order to save myself. *Save us.*

Like my father always says. You have two choices in life—you can either be the lamb...or the slaughterer.

Cain finally got tired of being the lamb.

My chest constricts, and I feel around for my cigarettes. I don't blame Cain for standing up for himself, but it sucks that Mrs. Miller got caught in the crossfire.

Cain didn't mean it—I remind myself. He had no other choice. It was her or us…and he chose us.

Just like I did.

"Yeah, I talked to him." Fetching my lighter, I put the flame to the end of my cigarette and take a long drag. "Listen, I don't know if you heard but—"

"Mrs. Miller's dead." His voice is flat. Devoid of any emotion… not even shock. "Her husband beat her to death."

"Yeah," I utter, the gravity of it all settling in my gut like a brick. "It su—"

"How did everything go at the precinct?"

His immediate change of subject sends a spike of irritation through me. "You mean apart from finding out Mrs. Miller died? Fine, I guess."

His heavy sigh tells me he's about as irritated as I am. "Did you stick to the story? Or did you throw a curveball like you usually do?"

I cross my arms. "I didn't throw any curveballs. I told you, I got your back."

"Why?"

My eyes narrow. I don't like that he's questioning my motives when he already knows he has my unconditional loyalty. Or how he won't spare Mrs. Miller's death more than a second of his time considering he's partially responsible for it.

And I'm feeling all kinds of fucked up about it.

Dragging a hand over my scalp, I mutter a curse. "You already know why, Cain."

"Because you're a cocksucker who's infatuated with me."

There's no teasing in his voice. It comes out like an accusation.

"Yeah, well. Last time I checked, your feelings were mutual."

With the way Cain's been on *my* dick lately, I thought he moved past his hang-ups about our situation.

I thought he realized, just like I did weeks ago—that what we have—this eerie pull between us—isn't wrong.

"Christ." His laugh is antagonizing. "You're either too stupid to realize, or too obsessed with me to notice."

The energy in the room transforms into something ominous and my muscles tense on instinct. "Realize what?"

"That two people can feel the same emotion for two *very* different reasons," he says slowly like I'm a small child incapable of comprehending something so extensive.

And fuck me, because I'm starting to feel like one. Cain's not being straightforward with me. He's speaking in riddles and then cutting me off with nasty remarks…like a politician having a debate with his opponent.

But I'm not Cain's opponent. *I've never been his opponent.* We're a team.

Before I can ask him what his problem is, the lights in the neon tank turn on. Usually, I have a divider between the regular fish and my piranha until he's ready to eat them.

But there aren't any regular fish. There's only my piranha in the main part of the tank…and what appears to be a new piranha on the other side of the divider.

"For instance, take these two piranhas," Cain states. "Your piranha has been fed today. He is calm. Relaxed. In control. But the other one? He's hungry, Damien. It's been so long since he's been fed, he's downright desperate. It doesn't even matter what kind of food he gets, or where it comes from…he'll do anything for it."

More riddles. More smoke screens. It's all I can do not to reach over and shake the shit out of him until he gives me something real.

Something that doesn't twist my insides like every word out of his mouth does currently.

"Is there a point—"

He clicks a button on the remote next to him. "Watch what happens when the two piranhas meet."

"Cain—" It's too late. The hungry piranha is already devouring the other one.

He never saw it coming.

Cain spins around to face me. "Two hungry piranhas can never coexist in one tank, Damien. Sooner or later, one will lose."

His expression twists. There's so much animosity radiating from him I nearly rock back on my feet. "Much like the piranha you kept on the other side of the divider…you stalked and salivated over me for weeks, waiting for the right opportunity to feast." He rises from the chair. "But when it didn't come fast enough, you decided to create your own by screwing my girlfriend —and then while I was at my lowest, you used the leverage you gained to lure me into your fucked-up playground." His eyes become tiny slits. "When I resisted, you seduced me with temptation and lust… utilizing Mrs. Miller as bait until I finally caved." He walks toward me slowly, sizing me up. "However, me participating in your bedroom games wasn't enough…because it wasn't what you really wanted. Our mock friendship was merely a trap. A divider that enabled you to get a closer look at your meal… because you weren't going to stop pursuing me until I was all yours."

Cain's not wrong. I needed to find out what made him tick…see if we were cut from the same cloth as I'd suspected.

But in order to find all that out, I had to invite him into my world and get under his skin like he'd gotten under mine.

I had to find out why my interest in him was becoming all-consuming. An unbearable itch that would kill me if I didn't scratch it.

And once I realized why…he didn't stand a chance in hell of escaping me. He was mine the moment I decided I wanted him to be.

Just like everyone else I've ever wanted. Only unlike them… Cain's special.

However, if Cain didn't want this, he could have stopped it before it spun out of control. Instead, he kept coming back for more.

Kept toying with me. Kept pushing my buttons.

Because he likes my attention. And he craves the things I do to his body.

He's addicted to his pedestal. Same way I'm addicted to him.

"You can stand here and point fingers at me. You can even make yourself believe you were taken advantage of if that's what helps you sleep at night." Taking a step forward, I close the distance between us. I smirk when I feel the growing bulge along his thigh. I haven't even touched him and he's already hard. "But we both know my interest wasn't one-sided. You enjoy being my prey." Leaning in, I lick the shell of his ear. "The only thing you didn't like? Was the idea of sharing your pedestal with someone else. Which is why you got rid of Mrs. Miller."

"You're right." The sound of his zipper lowering has my own dick hardening. "It's no secret I've always had a problem sharing my toys and getting along with others."

The bitterness in his tone is unmistakable. I want to remind him this is no longer a competition because Mrs. Miller's already dead and I'm already his—but he presses down on my shoulder, urging me on my knees. "Now why don't you give me something to take the edge off while I finish the rest of this conversation?"

I shake my head. "Conversation is already over." Gripping his neck, I lean my forehead against his. "And I'm not in the mood to suck your dick." I sink my teeth into his lower lip and slip my other hand down the back of his pants. "I want to tie you up and fuck you so hard you won't be able to walk for weeks."

His nostrils flare as I begin prepping him with my finger, and I can see the internal war he's waging with himself. It's almost cute, considering we both know I'll be balls deep inside his ass in the next minute. He can't resist me any more than I can resist him.

"Damien." His voice is a low rasp, almost pleading. "Please."

And just like that…I'm caving and dropping to my knees for him.

Cain's out of sorts and it's obvious he needs me. I'm willing to put my selfish needs aside momentarily and give him what he wants.

His hand goes to my head as I pull him out. "I knew you'd give in." He groans as I proceed to tease him. "You're so fucking obsessed you'd do anything for me, huh?"

Being submissive has never been my thing, but what's happening in this moment is beyond that. It's about being partners—one taking care of the other when they're spinning out.

If Cain needs me to relinquish control in order to get some of it back so he can feel better—I'll do it.

He groans my name when I take him in my mouth. "I bet you'd even let me fuck you if I wanted to."

I freeze. The idea of Cain screwing me has never appealed to me before and it doesn't now.

He strokes my cheek. "Wouldn't you, Damien?"

I nod in agreement.

This is what happens when you meet your match. You sacrifice the things you want…or in this case, don't want…for the things they do.

A grin tugs at the corners of his lips. "I wonder what else you'd let me do?"

"Anything you want."

I mean it. Cain needs to know we're not rivals. We never were. We're equals. No…more than that. *We're a team.*

He's mine and I'm his.

Taking him deeper, I go back to the task at hand. Drawing out little grunts of pleasure from Cain that go straight to my own cock.

"I'd bet you'd let me tie *you* up," he rasps. "Let me make you my sex slave, fulfilling my every command because you're so desperate for me."

I suck him harder and he trembles, thrusting his hips into my face. "Wouldn't you, Damien?"

Releasing him, I look up. "If that's what you wanted."

He yanks my shirt over my head and shakes it out before he tosses it across the room. "What I want right now is to fuck you. Take off your pants."

"Wait," he says when I start undoing my belt.

"What?"

His eyes darken. "I have to pee." An evil grin spreads across his face and he runs the tip of his dick along my bottom lip. "Open."

The organ in my chest beats so hard it hurts. I know this is nothing more than a power play. A way for Cain to see how loyal I truly am…how far I'm willing to go for him.

Not breaking eye contact, I part my lips and hold my breath. Preparing for what's to come.

His callous laugh confuses me. "God, you're fucking pathetic. No wonder your mother was a dope head. She needed an escape from her slow, moronic son." He pushes my head away. "You're so obsessed with me. So desperate for my dick…you failed to realize what was really happening between us."

I'm trying to wrap my head around what he's saying and what it means, but Cain's fifty steps ahead of me in what feels like a millisecond. "Failed to realize what exactly?"

"This whole time you thought I was your prey…but you were mine." He pulls something out of his pocket. A small black cassette tape. "It was nice being fawned over, having my dick sucked whenever I wanted, and of course—having an alibi when I needed one. But our time together is over, Damien. There's only room for one of us in this tank."

I open my mouth to speak, but he presses a button on the phone and my voice fills the room.

"*Well, before the pills, I would have re-wired an everyday household item...something simple…maybe a coffee maker or toaster. This way, they'd blame it on faulty wiring.*"

"Blame what on faulty wiring?"

"The fire that would kill him."

His smile is as cruel as he is. "Our paths might have crossed, but my future plans don't include you."

I stand up, which is a bad idea because the room is spinning. I'm trying to connect the dots…no that's wrong. I've already connected the dots—it wasn't hard—but my brain is trying to make up excuses as to why he did it.

Even though my heart already knows the truth.

This isn't a mistake or a lapse in judgment. He recorded that conversation for one reason and one reason only.

To set me up to take the fall.

And that can only mean one thing. Cain never felt the same way for me as I do for him. He just wanted me to believe he did.

My partner. The object of my fascination…the person I thought was my reward for all the bad shit I've been through…is a traitor.

And I was nothing more than a love-sick pawn.

This whole time I thought Cain made me a better person…but it was only because I made him a worse one.

Just like my piranha who ended up a meal just moments prior. I didn't realize I was in danger until it was too late.

The sound of the gun cocking is loud in the now quiet room. Cain's not even shaking as he points it at me. If anything, he's calm and collected.

He's in total control. Blowing me off the face of this earth doesn't impact him in the least.

And why should it…his body count is already up to three. What's one more to a psychopath?

"You have three choices." His eyes flash. "Option one—I can kill you and make it look like you took your own life because your *guilt* about being a murderer was starting to eat you alive." He shrugs. "It's not a bad way to go. People will still hate you, but at least they'll know you felt remorse for your sins at the end."

A surge of anger rushes through me and I press my forehead into the gun he's holding against it. "What are you waiting for? Pull the fucking trigger."

He's already stripped me of everything I've ever cared about in the last five minutes…including my power and control. He might as well finish me off.

He clicks his tongue. "Option two—I could call Detective Trejo and tell him I stumbled upon a certain recording that I found in my brother's car…and you can go to jail for the rest of your life." He winks. "Come to think of it, you might like it there. It's not all that different from your life now. Minus the fish tank of course. You'll still have plenty of time to work out and fuck."

I stay silent, the rage inside me waging war with the sharp pain of Cain's betrayal.

"What's option three?"

It doesn't make sense why he'd give me another option when it's clear there are only two.

His expression doesn't change. "I'll let you live…but it will be in torment. If you choose option three—you will walk out your front door in the next minute and never step foot in this town again, or even think about contacting me for the rest of your miserable life. Because if you do? I'm picking option one or two."

Option three is the worst one of them all.

My throat burns. "Ca—

The sound of the gun firing makes my ears ring and for a moment, I'm thankful he shot me.

Only he didn't. He shot the wall behind me. "Get the fuck out, Damien."

I don't move a muscle. If he's going to break my heart and screw up my life, the least he can do is have the guts to end it on my terms.

Because I don't want to live in the four walls of a prison cell without my freedom like one of my mother's fish in captivity.

And I sure as fuck don't want to live in a world where I can't have him.

"Option one."

For a second, I see something pass in his gaze, but then it's gone when he reaches in his pocket with his free hand and pulls out his cell.

I watch in outrage as he brings it to his ear. "Hey, Detective Trejo. It's Cain Carter. Listen—"

"I'll leave."

As usual. I'm at his mercy. He's making the choice for me.

He hangs up the phone. "You have twenty seconds."

Bending down, I pick up my shirt, holding out hope that he'll tell me this is nothing more than a stupid joke and he just wanted to see how far I'd go for him.

"Cain." Despite the gun he's holding, I edge forward. As close as I can get to him. Maybe he needs to hear someone say it. Just like I do.

"I love—"

A stream of warm liquid saturates my clothes before a faint ammonia smell fills my nostrils. I look down in shock.

Cain's peeing on me…like he's a dog and I'm a goddamn fire hydrant.

"You have two seconds to leave me the fuck alone forever, or I'll call Detective Trejo back." The gun in his hand shakes as he continues urinating, aiming for my pants and shoes. "I never wanted you, and I sure as hell never loved you, you fucking faggot. I never will."

The heart I wasn't sure I had until Cain, shatters as I run out of my bedroom. Leaving nothing but a gaping hole in my chest.

A gaping hole now filled with a venomous wrath so strong, I start shaking with the force of it.

If Cain thought I was obsessed before, he has no idea what kind of poison his hurt and betrayal has unleashed inside of me.

Sometimes the only difference between love and obsession is a broken heart.

And unfortunately for Cain…there's no longer love.

There's only darkness. A need for vengeance.

But it's not enough to idly threaten him. It's not enough to screw with his head.

No…I'm going to bide my time and let Cain lead his perfect life.

I'm going to let him forget about me.

And then…when he's content and happy. When he's close to getting everything he ever wanted.

When he finally falls in love…or at the very least, a lust so powerful it drives him crazy with obsession.

That's when I'll appear.

Because the best way to hurt someone, the *only* way to make them truly pay and suffer for their sins…is to strike when they least expect it.

And then destroy everything they ever wanted…everything they ever cared about.

Until they have nothing.

Preview
THE DEVIL'S ADVOCATE

Chapter 1 (Eden)

It's not Cain. It can't be.

Cain wouldn't bring me here just so he could hurt me like this.

He loves me.

I wipe the tear making its way down my cheek with my fingers.

Despite my brain's insistence that the man leaving in a haste isn't Cain…another tear falls.

His lips.

Everything else about the man. His hair, his tux, even the way he touched the woman he kissed on the dancefloor…I could chalk up to coincidence. But I know those lips.

They're the same lips I've dreamed about kissing since I was fourteen.

But my heart isn't convinced. It needs proof. I refuse to believe Cain would betray me like this.

I take a step forward, preparing to follow him out of the ballroom, but the ground beneath me tilts and I stumble instead.

I'm trying to gather my bearings when the lights above me change colors, illuminating the room in a red glow.

"Take it easy, sweetheart." The man next to me nods at the now packed dance floor. "Cocktail hour just ended, and you're already hammered."

I blink in confusion. *I'm not drunk.* Anxiety shoots through me like a rocket and I clutch my chest. It's becoming an actual struggle to draw in air.

Oh, God. I'm having a panic attack. Right here in front of all these people.

"Why don't we go somewhere more private for a little while?" the man shouts in my ear, so loud I wince. "This way I can look after you."

The man tugs on my hand, but I yank it back.

Nausea churns my insides. I need to get out of here but my feet won't move, no matter how much I plead with them to.

Cain. I need him. He's the only one who can help me through this.

Instinctively, I peruse the room for him while I pull out my phone, ignoring the little voice inside mocking my efforts.

Angelbaby123: I feel like I'm going to pass out. I'm on the dancefloor.

I think I spot him, but strobe lights start flickering, and the music changes—filling my ears with uneven beats, dark harmonies, and intense tempos.

My senses kick into overdrive, making it impossible to concentrate, but I scan the room in a last-ditch attempt anyway and send a text directly to his phone instead of the app.

Eden: Please, Cain. I need you.

"Fine, be that way," the man next to me snaps. "I was only trying to help, you drunk bitch."

"What?" I can't understand a word he's saying. I want to ask him to repeat himself, but the lights flash…and then it's nothing but darkness.

A few people scream, but it's drowned out by a spooky, evil laugh that crackles through the speakers.

A moment later, the lights turn back on, sheathing the room in a blood red hue again.

My legs finally get the signal and I put one foot in front of the other. I'm halfway to the exit when the lights go out for a second time. It's so dark I can't even make out shapes, let alone walk.

Terror spirals through me when a muscular arm wraps around my waist.

I open my mouth to yell at the asshole who won't take no for an answer, but I'm slammed against a wall.

"Wh—" My eyes adjust, enabling me to see the tall figure wearing a black mask in front of me. My heart takes flight when I inhale the scent of Cain's aftershave.

"Cain." I smile, feeling both relieved he came to my rescue and stupid for ever thinking he would bring me here to hurt me. "You found—" My voice catches when he presses his palm over my heart. The part of me he owns and controls. The part of me that will forever be tethered to him.

I look down when his hand compresses, painfully constricting the organ. "What are you doing?"

I try to maneuver out of his hold, but he's too strong. Whenever I inhale, he pushes down harder. Fear pumps through my veins and I grip the collar of his jacket, urging him to stop.

White spots form in front of my eyes and the hand gripping his collar goes limp at my side. It physically hurts to breathe. I'm going to pass out if he doesn't let up in the next ten seconds.

I flatten my back against the wall, hoping to catch a shallow breath, but the crushing weight becomes so unbearable, I give up.

My knees buckle and I start to fall—but suddenly the force is gone.

I suck in air so fast I cough, and try to push him away, but he leans in, his mouth hovering over my ear. "Remember that feeling, Eden." His voice is deep and raspy…different. "Because it's only going to get worse."

My blood runs cold. *It's not Cain.*

"Who are you?"

I feel his lips curve against the shell of my ear. "A friend."

My cheeks heat when he nuzzles my neck and plants a kiss where my pulse is beating erratically. "My friends don't hurt me."

I know I should be running away and finding Cain, but I need to know who this man is and how he knows my name.

And why my body responds to him the way it does…even though it's obvious he wants to harm me.

"You're right." His teeth scrape my flesh as his hand slips through the slit in my dress. "I'm definitely *not* your friend." The vehemence in his tone is chilling, yet his touch is soft like velvet. "Consider me a messenger." He gives me an evil grin that makes my stomach drop. "Cain's waiting for you upstairs."

I blink in confusion. "Cain sent you to get me?"

That doesn't seem right, although it's not entirely out of the question. Cain has people to do his bidding for him. But it's weird that he would send one of his employees to fetch me.

The tip of his finger slithers up my thigh and I glare at him. "I suggest you keep your hands to yourself, *Sir*. Because if Cain ever finds out you touched me, I guarantee you'll be out of a job." I crinkle my nose. "And probably a few teeth."

He smirks. "It's a shame we didn't meet under different circumstances." He captures my hand with his free one and kisses my finger. The one I cut on broken glass. "Last bedroom on the second floor." He plucks the string of pearls against my hip bone. "The one next to the closet."

With that, he releases me.

Grab the Final Book here

Cards of Love Collection

The Devil is just one of the many stories in the Cards of Love Collection. Which card will you choose next?
www.cardsofloveromance.com

Acknowledgments

There's honestly no way I can possibly thank each and every one of you. You're all amazing and supportive and I can't do any of this without you.

Willow Winters: Thank you for letting me be apart of such an amazing experience and for believing in me. You are the sweetheart of the indie world, and if everyone in the world were even half as sweet as you are, it would be a much better place.

Avery: I don't know what else I can say to you that hasn't already been said. As always you carried me through this process and I'm so thankful for you. Thank you for holding my hand and being objective when I couldn't. Thank you for always encouraging me and being there for me.

Kristy: I can't thank you enough. Thank you for letting helping me out of my creative spiral and letting me talk and plot your ear off and untangling my brain when I was going crazy. I'm pretty sure I'd still be sitting at my desk having a panic attack over whether or not I could put my big girl panties on, pull the trigger, and write the damn story if it wasn't for you.

Brandi, Vickie, Jackie, Crystal, Rebecca, Shonda, Mary, Beth, Dee, Jodie, Kris, and Michelle my NY friend.

You all have been *vital* to this process. Thank you so much for trusting me and giving me your input. Thank you for being there at all hours of the morning (or night) and putting everything aside to read my words. Thank you for your continued support and for being my cheerleaders. <3

Ellie: I love your face. I'm keeping you. Thank you for everything. I know it's not easy working with my schedule and I know I probably drive you crazy. Thank you for dealing with me and thank you for working with me.

Lori—Thank you for such a gorgeous cover!

My reader group—I have the best *Angry Girls* on the planet. I love you all so much. Thank you for all of your support and giving me someplace where I can be me and connect with all of you. You guys rock.

Last, but not least—to all the amazing ***Cards of Love*** author-sisters.

Readers,

Please—read them, Fall in love with them. And tell everyone you know about them. They are immensely talented, and they work their butts off to bring you stories you love (*even if their characters make you want to throw your kindle sometimes.*) These authors don't just bring you words on a page. They bring you stories that will break your heart in one chapter only to mend it the next. Stories that drive you outside your boxes (and usually your comfort zone). Stories that challenge you. Heal you. Stories that make you laugh. Make you cry. Inspire you. Make you angry. Make you swoon.

Stories that never fail to always make you feel.

So please—review our books, spread the word, and share your knowledge of them with others. Because knowledge is power.

And readers are incredibly powerful. <3

About the Author

Want to be notified about my upcoming releases? https://goo.gl/n5Azwv

Ashley Jade craves tackling different genres and tropes within romance. Her first loves are New Adult Romance and Romantic Suspense, but she also writes everything in between including: contemporary romance, erotica, and dark romance.

Her characters are flawed and complex, and chances are you will hate them before you fall head over heels in love with them.

She's a die-hard lover of oxford commas, em dashes, music, coffee, and anything thought provoking...except for math.

Books make her heart beat faster and writing makes her soul come alive. She's always read books growing up and scribbled stories in her journal, and after having a strange dream one night; she decided to just go for it and publish her first series.

It was the best decision she ever made.

If she's not paying off student loan debt, working, or writing a novel—you can usually find her listening to music, hanging out with her readers online, and pondering the meaning of life.

Check out her social media pages for future novels.

She recently became hip and joined Twitter, so you can find her there, too.

She loves connecting with her readers—they make her world go round'.

~Happy Reading~

~

Feel free to email her with any questions / comments: ashleyjadeauthor@gmail.com

For more news about what I'm working on next: Follow me on my Facebook page: https://www.facebook.-com/pages/Ashley-Jade/788137781302982

Other Books Written By Ashley Jade

Royal Hearts Academy Series (Books 1-4)
Cruel Prince (Jace's Book)
Ruthless Knight (Cole's Book)
Wicked Princess (Bianca's Book)
Broken Kingdom

Hate Me - Standalone

The Devil's Playground Duet (Books 1 & 2)

Complicated Parts Series (Books 1-3)

Complicated Hearts - Duet (Books 1 & 2)

Blame It on the Shame - Trilogy (Parts 1-3)

Blame It on the Pain - Standalone

~

Thanks for Reading!
Please follow me online for more.
<3 Ashley Jade